"WHAT IS THE ERRAND?"

A Little Maid

OF

Old Connecticut

BY

ALICE TURNER CURTIS

AUTHOR OF

A LITTLE MAID OF OLD NEW YORK
A LITTLE MAID OF OLD PHILADELPHIA
A LITTLE MAID OF MASSACHUSETTS COLONY
A LITTLE MAID OF MARYLAND

ILLUSTRATED BY WUANITA SMITH

APPLEWOOD BOOKS
BEDFORD, MASSACHUSETTS

A Little Maid of Old Connecticut was first published by the Penn Publishing Company in 1918.

ISBN 1-55709-328-8

Thank you for purchasing an Applewood Book.
Applewood reprints America's lively classics—
books from the past that are still of interest to modern readers.
For a free copy of our current catalog, write to:
Applewood Books, Box 365, Bedford, MA 01730.

10 9 8 7 6 5 4 3 2

Printed and bound in Canada.

Library of Congress Cataloging-in-Publication Data
Curtis, Alice Turner.
    A little maid of old Connecticut / by Alice Turner Curtis;
illustrated by Wuanita Smith.
        p.   cm.
    Summary: In 1776 a young Connecticut girl, unaware that her
hat box contains a mysterious package from a Tory prisoner, trav-
els by stagecoach to visit her grandmother.
    ISBN 1-55709-328-8
    1. United States—History—Revolution, 1775–1783—Juvenile
fiction.   [1. United States—History—Revolution, 1775–1783—
Fiction.   2. Connecticut—Fiction.]
I. Smith, Wuanita, ill.   II. Title
PZ7.C941Lmt   1996
[Fic]–dc20   96-28381
                                       CIP
                                        AC

Introduction

LITTLE Ellen Elizabeth Barlow lived in Connecticut in the troublous days of 1777, when enemy war vessels and Tory bands were ravaging the coast settlements of the Colony. The first time she ever left her home was when she took a stage-coach at her father's door and traveled down to Hartford to visit her grandmother, carrying her new silk bonnet in a bandbox. Something else was slipped into the box, also—a mysterious package from a Tory prisoner, which caused the little girl some anxious hours before Governor Jonathan Trumbull set her mind at rest.

Each of the other books of this series, *A Little Maid of Provincetown*, *A Little Maid of Massachusetts Colony*, *A Little Maid of Old New York*, *A Little Maid of Old Philadelphia*, *A Little Maid of Maryland*, *A Little Maid of Ticonderoga*, also tells the story of a girl in the days of the American Revolution that cannot fail to interest young patriots of to-day.

Contents

Illustrations

A Little Maid of Old Connecticut

CHAPTER I

MISS ELLEN ELIZABETH BARLOW

ELLIE BARLOW stood just inside the gate watching for the big coach, on its way to Hartford, which passed her father's house every Thursday morning. She could see the horses when they came over the top of the hill, and then the big yellow coach, with its load of passengers, and with boxes and bundles securely strapped on behind.

The driver of the coach seemed a very fine person to the little girl. He wore a round hat turned up in front. His coat was green, with big shining brass buttons, and he flourished a long whip, the lash of which could reach the leaders of the four horses that brought the coach over the road at such a good pace.

It was usually about eleven o'clock in the morning when the coach passed; and by half-past ten Ellie was at the gate. Mr. Samuel Pettigrew, the driver, always waved his gloved hand to the little girl, and Ellie waved back, and then watched the coach until a distant hill hid it from view. Then she would go slowly back to the house, wishing that she might some day go driving grandly off to Hartford, a passenger in the coach.

But this morning in early June of 1776 Ellie watched the coach with a new delight. "Just think," she whispered to herself, "when next Thursday comes the coach will stop at this very gate, and the steps will be let down, and I shall get in the coach and be riding off to Hartford." And at the thought of this wonderful adventure so near at hand, Ellie gave a little jump of delight, and ran back to the house, her black curls dancing in the air and her dark eyes eager with anticipation.

The Barlow farm was a half day's ride from Hartford, on the main road which led to Salisbury. It was a brown, weather-beaten house, and stood well back from the road. There was a big oak tree nearly in front of the house, and on the slope behind grew many apple trees. Ellie was sure that the Barlow farm was the finest farm in all Connecticut.

She had heard older people say that it raised the best flax in the county; and that no one had such prosperous flocks of sheep as Mr. David Barlow; and Ellie knew that she should always want to live there; but, nevertheless, it was a delightful thing to have a grandmother in the fine town of Hartford who had invited you to come for a visit. Ellie's mother had been born in Hartford, and had told her little daughter many stories about its brick mansion-houses, its shops and churches. The little girl knew that ships were built in Hartford. Her own mother had been on one when it was launched, years ago. And Grandmother Hinman lived near the market-place, where coaches could be seen every day in the week, and where you could hear the bells of three churches on every Sunday morning. No wonder the little girl could hardly wait for the day set for her journey.

Ellie ran straight to the kitchen, where her mother was preparing the midday meal.

"I was just going to call you, Ellie. The table is not set; and there is your father coming up from the meadow, and the boys will be here before we are ready."

As Mrs. Barlow spoke she drew the table toward the center of the big, pleasant kitchen, and Ellie helped spread the white home-made table-cloth, and put on the heavy earthenware plates, and the pewter mugs, and ran to the cellar for the golden butter and a pitcher of cool milk.

"Just think, mother, in another week I shall be on my way to Hartford in the coach!" said Ellie as she set down the pitcher.

"Yes, dear; and this very afternoon I must take the linen from the loom and cut you out a dress. You will have to make it yourself, for I want to make you a frock of the flecked silk that your father brought home from his last trip to Hartford."

"Truly! Oh, mother! I am sure grandmother will think I have too many fine things!" declared Ellie, remembering her hat of braided straw, which she had helped to make and which her mother had trimmed with a wide blue ribbon, and of another even more beautiful hat of pale blue shirred silk which was carefully put away in the big bandbox in an upper room.

"Here's father now!" and Ellie ran toward the open door, and a second later her father had lifted her in his arms and swung her up so high that her head touched the low ceiling.

"Oh, father! I'm too big now to be swung about," she said, as he lowered her to the floor.

"So you are. Big enough to go off on a journey all by yourself," her father responded laughingly. Then his face grew more serious. "I have half a mind to go with the child," he said, turning toward his wife. "But I may be called to my regiment any day now."

Before Mrs. Barlow could reply two boys came running into the kitchen.

"Dinner ready?" they exclaimed together.

"Yes, indeed, and waiting," responded Mrs. Barlow, smiling at her tall sons. Stephen, the eldest, was nearly sixteen years old, and Will was two years younger. They were both tall for their age, with dark eyes and hair like their sister's. They were already a great help to their father, and always ready and watchful to assist their mother in the work of the house. Stephen was quite sure that he was old enough to enlist.

It was nearly a year after the Battle of Bunker Hill, and no colony was more interested in the success of the American cause than Connecticut. She had sent help to beleaguered Boston, and many boys but little older than Stephen were bearing arms. And it was a gloomy outlook for Connecticut just then. The British were near, and every citizen realized that he must be ready to defend his home.

As the little family gathered about the table they all bowed their heads for the brief grace which Mr. Barlow never omitted.

Will was greatly interested in the growth of some mulberry trees which he had planted two years before, for the purpose of raising silkworms.

"It won't be long before we'll be making silk enough for you and Ellen to have all the dresses you want, that is, if I can only get silkworms," he announced, as he told his mother of the rapid growth of the mulberry trees.

"Something else to think about besides silk dresses and mulberry trees," grumbled Stephen, passing his plate for a second helping of the roast lamb. "Mayn't I go to Hartford with Ellie?" he continued, looking from his mother to his father with hopeful eyes; for in Hartford, as Stephen well knew, there were always soldiers arriving home or starting forth; captured Tories were being brought in under guard, and it seemed to Stephen that nothing but the American cause for Liberty was worth thinking about.

"Don't ask that question again, Stephen," his father answered. "You know I may have to leave any day. You are needed here, to help your mother and protect the farm."

"No fear of the British coming this way," declared Stephen, not ill-pleased that his father should think of him as able to defend his home.

"I can go alone. The stage-driver will look out for me," said Ellie, half fearing that after all her father might decide to keep her at home.

"Yes, you will be quite safe," agreed Mrs. Barlow. "You will be in Hartford before supper time, and your grandma will be looking for you."

"I expect Mr. Pettigrew will be surprised when he sees me all ready to get into the coach," said Ellie, smiling happily as she looked across the table toward her father.

"Did you wish to surprise him, Ellie? If you did I have spoiled your plan; for I told him that my daughter, Miss Ellen Elizabeth Barlow, would be a passenger on Thursday; and for him to be sure to stop at our gate," responded her father.

Ellie was evidently delighted.

"Oh, father! Then he will be surprised. Of course he will think that 'Miss Ellen Elizabeth Barlow' must be a grown-up young lady, and when he sees me—" and Ellie laughed aloud at the thought of the surprise in store for the stage-driver.

"I mean to tell him to take great care of you. It is quite a journey for a little girl only ten years old," said Mr. Barlow.

"Nothing could befall the child, unless she can manage to fall out of the window," declared Ellen's mother. "We shall see her safely started, and her grandmother will be watching for the arrival of the coach. You must not make her fearful, David."

"Sometimes I think all my children have too much courage," responded Mr. Barlow, nodding toward Stephen. "The boys are sure they could defeat a regiment of trained soldiers; and I don't think Ellie knows what fear is."

"Oh, yes, I do, father! Wasn't I afraid every time the teacher spoke to me all last term," replied the little girl, who had not been very happy at school, and was now delighted to hear that the school was to have a new teacher when it opened for the autumn term.

After dinner Ellie helped her mother wash the dishes.

"Shall I help Grandmother Hinman when I am at her house?" Ellie asked, as she gave the shining pewter mugs a careful rub.

"Perhaps grandma may find something for you to do; but I suppose Hannah Jane will hardly let you step foot in her kitchen," Mrs. Barlow answered, smiling at the remembrance of the sturdy old Scotchwoman who had been a helper in the Hinman family when Mrs. Barlow herself was no older than Ellie.

There was another question which Ellie wanted very much to ask, but she had resolved not to. She wanted, more than anything, to know if there would be any little girls who lived near her grandmother's house, and who would come and see her. For the Barlows had no near neighbors, and Ellie had no girl friends of her own age. The schoolhouse was two miles distant, and the girls with whom Ellie became acquainted at school all lived beyond the schoolhouse; so when school closed for the long vacation she often did not see them for months.

"You will have four little girls for neighbors at grandmother's," said Mrs. Barlow, as Ellie followed her mother into the big front living-room, where stood the small hand-loom on which was the checked gingham for Ellie's new dress.

Ellie stood in the doorway. "Oh, mother!" she exclaimed. "Four little girls!"

"Why, yes; have I not told you about the Chaplin children? Bertha and Mildred are the two oldest. Bertha is twelve, and Mildred is just your age. And Nancy is eight, while little Lucy is only six."

"Four little girls!" repeated Ellie with such delight in her voice that her mother looked at her in surprise.

"I was wishing and wishing that there would be little girls at grandmother's!" declared Ellie. "It seems just as if I was going to have everything. Why! Just going in the coach was enough!" and she stopped as if so many delights were more than she could realize.

"Yes, dear; you are sure to have a happy visit. And now I will take the gingham from the loom and cut out your dress. Bring your work-bag, for you must stitch up the seams this afternoon," responded her mother; and Ellie ran into the hall and up the narrow twisting stairs to her room after the pretty little work-bag which held her thimble, scissors and needles. She was eager to ask her mother about the little Chaplin girls, and as she drew the rocking-chair, which her brothers had made for her on her last birthday, near one of the sitting-room windows and sat down to wait for the work which her mother was basting, she said:

"Now tell me about the little Chaplin girls, mother. And do you think they will come and see me every day?"

Mrs. Barlow laughed as she looked toward Ellie.

"Why, my dear, I have told you all I know about them. It is what your grandmother wrote in her letter.

Very likely you will see them every day; but you must remember not to go to their house except when they invite you."

"Oh, mother! They might want me to come and forget to ask me," said Ellie.

"Yes, so they might. But that would be their affair. And in big towns like Hartford little visitors must always wait to be invited," responded Mrs. Barlow.

"I'll remember," Ellie promised smilingly. She was quite sure that the four little Chaplin girls would ask her to come every day.

CHAPTER II

STEPHEN'S PRISONER

THERE was a tall rose-bush near the window where Ellie sat sewing up the seams in the pretty brown-checked gingham, which her mother had woven on the hand-loom. The rose-bush had been brought, as a tiny slip, from Grandmother Hinman's garden when Ellie's mother married and came to live on the Barlow farm. When Ellie was a very small girl, not more than five or six years old, she had announced one day that the "yellow rose-bush," was hers, and that no one was to pick a rose from it without her permission, and the other members of the family had good-naturedly agreed.

"If it is your property then you must take care of it," her mother had said; and Ellie was shown how to trim off the dead wood, and had learned that soap-suds thrown over the leaves and branches kept them clear from bugs. Every autumn she brought leaves from under the big oak tree, and branches of spruce from the pasture and "banked up" her rose-bush to protect it from the icy cold and frost of winter. Each year the tree had grown and flourished, and it was now full of

19

yellow blossoms which sent a pleasant fragrance through the open windows.

"I can take some of my roses to grandmother," said Ellie, "and then I can see if they are really so fine and large as Hartford roses."

"You must ask your grandmother to tell you the story of her rose-tree," said Mrs. Barlow.

"You tell me, mother," Ellie responded. But Mrs. Barlow shook her head.

"No, my dear; grandma can tell it much better than I can, and it is a story well worth listening to. But I will tell you this much: Grandma's rose tree, of which yours is a slip, came from Holyrood Castle in Edinburgh, Scotland."

"And is that why it is a Scotch rose?" Ellie asked.

"Grandmother will tell you all about it," replied her mother; and Ellie instantly resolved to find out the history of her rose-tree the very night of her arrival in Hartford. It seemed to the little girl that every day and hour was bringing some new delight and interest in the visit to Grandmother Hinman.

"Oh, mother! What is that?" Ellie exclaimed suddenly, jumping up from her chair, and dropping her work on the floor.

Mrs. Barlow did not answer, for she also had sprung to her feet and was now moving toward the window.

"It was a shot, wasn't it, mother?" Ellie half whispered; for it was a time when every household along the Connecticut River feared a possible attack from the invader's troops; and the sound of a musket-shot might mean serious trouble. Farmers often took their guns with them in the fields, and it was no wonder that Mrs. Barlow and Ellie were frightened and alarmed.

"Mother, mayn't I run to the meadow and call father?" Ellie asked.

But her mother shook her head, and an instant later Will came running across the field. He was waving his straw hat as if in triumph, and before he reached the house he called out: "Steve has captured a Tory."

"For pity's sake!" exclaimed Mrs. Barlow, hastening to meet him, closely followed by Ellie.

"Here they come. Look!" and Will pointed toward the lower field.

"Where's your father? Who fired the gun?" questioned Mrs. Barlow.

"The Tory fired the gun. Father's coming," said Will, fairly dancing up and down in his excitement.

As Stephen and his prisoner came nearer Mrs. Barlow exclaimed again: "Why, he isn't much older than Stevie!" for the red-coated prisoner who limped along, his hands fastened together, and his own gun held by Stephen, was evidently a boy not over eighteen or twenty. Mr. Barlow was close behind the captive, and apparently more amused than alarmed by the affair.

Stephen's face was flushed with pride. He felt that he was at last really helping the American cause.

"Did he shoot at you, Stevie?" Ellie whispered fearfully, running along by her brother's side.

"I don't know what he *thought* he was shooting at. The bullet struck the top of the fence," Stephen answered scornfully.

Ellie looked at her brother's prisoner with wondering eyes. She had never seen a Tory soldier before, and it seemed to her very queer that any one could be afraid of a boy who looked so much like the boys of Connecticut. The prisoner had brown hair, which had evidently not been combed or cut for a long time; his fair skin was burned and freckled, and his uniform worn and soiled. A bare toe stuck through the old shoe, and he limped as if utterly worn out.

"Give me the gun, Stephen," said Mr. Barlow, coming forward, "and take the boy up to your room and let him lie down. He's very nearly exhausted. You and Will can stand guard over him," he concluded, seeing the look of disappointment on Stephen's face.

"All right, sir," responded Steve, in what he believed to be a very gruff and soldier-like tone.

"I believe the chap's about starved," Will found a chance to whisper to his mother as they entered the kitchen.

For a moment Mrs. Barlow hesitated. To give food to a man who was fighting against America's rights, who had, as she believed, fired his musket at her son, seemed for a moment more than she could do; but at that moment Stephen quickly reached out his arm. His prisoner had lurched forward, and but for Steve's help would have fallen.

"He hasn't spoken since we found him," said Will. "I believe he's ill," and as he spoke Will began to untie the stout cord with which Steve had fastened the stranger's hands, and Ellie ran to the well to bring in a pitcher of cool water.

It proved that the prisoner was really ill. His hands and head were burning with fever, and Mr. Barlow and Stephen had to carry him up-stairs and put him to bed. Mrs. Barlow started the kitchen fire and prepared a delicate broth, and all the family were now busy and interested in trying to help and aid one whom they knew to be their enemy. Stephen insisted on staying in the same room with his prisoner, and a cot was put up for him, although he declared that he should not close his eyes for the night.

"What really happened, David?" questioned Mrs. Barlow when she returned to the kitchen after having fed the young Tory, and left Stephen in charge of his prisoner.

"Why, I don't think anything really happened," Mr. Barlow replied. "This young redcoat was evidently hiding in the woods near the river, and when Stephen caught a glimpse of him and rushed toward him calling out, 'Surrender,' the fellow fired off his musket and fell over, just as he did here. I believe he is a deserter from the British Army who has been hiding until he is so worn out and nearly starved that he don't care what happens to him," concluded Mr. Barlow.

"Did he fire at Stevie?" asked Ellie.

"I don't believe he knew what he fired at. But it was his last charge of powder," said Mr. Barlow, who was examining the stranger's musket and powder-horn. "By Jove!" he exclaimed suddenly. "This is queer. Here is my name on this powder-horn, 'David Barlow,'" and he held it toward his wife, pointing to a small silver plate on which the name was engraved.

"But your powder-horn hasn't any name on it," said Will.

"This belongs to the young Tory. His name must be the same as mine," explained his father.

"Then he can't really be a Tory if his name is Barlow. But what made Stevie run at him before he knew whether he had a gun or not?" said Ellie.

"Stephen doesn't stop for a second thought when he sees a redcoat," responded her father; "a little military training would teach him more sense."

They were all now greatly interested to know more about the boy, who was in Stephen's room sound asleep.

For a time Ellie entirely forgot about her visit. She had no cousins named Barlow, and she wondered if the boy up-stairs might not prove to be a cousin. She knew that her Grandfather Barlow had been born in England.

"Now, Ellie, you must return to your sewing," her mother reminded her when Mr. Barlow and Will had gone back to their work in the field, "and your father thinks it best for us not to speak of this boy up-stairs, in case any neighbor or stranger comes this way."

"But Tories do not come this way, and Americans would be glad that he was here," replied Ellie.

"Yes, dear, that may be true; but until the boy is stronger and we know more about him we will not speak of Stevie's prisoner," replied her mother; and Ellie went slowly back to her little chair by the window, picked up the gingham, put on her little steel thimble and began to sew. But her thoughts were no longer on the story of the yellow rose-tree in Grandmother Hinman's garden, nor did she think of the little Chaplin girls who were to be her playmates; she was wondering about the sick boy up-stairs whose name was the same as that of her father.

"I don't believe he will ever be a Tory soldier again," she thought; "perhaps he didn't want to be. I hope he will tell us all about himself to-morrow."

But the young Tory was too ill to be questioned the next morning, and it was Mrs. Barlow who now took charge of Steve's prisoner, and not until the third day after his capture did he apparently realize that he was not hiding away from every human being.

"Did you call me 'David'?" he asked, looking up at Mrs. Barlow as she fed him with Steve's own silver spoon.

"Why, yes, I suppose I did. It is your name, isn't it?" she responded.

The boy smiled and nodded, and finished the broth with evident appetite. That afternoon he was bolstered up in bed, and was evidently much better.

When Mrs. Barlow told him that his name was the same as their own, he seemed greatly surprised and interested, and said that his home was near Exeter in England. But he said nothing more about himself, and Mrs. Barlow did not question him. She was very sure that when he was stronger, and realized that they were ready to be his friends, that this English boy would tell them his story.

"I'll take him to Hartford as soon as he is well," Stephen declared, when his mother told him of his captive's improvement.

"But he was running away from the Tory Army, Stevie," said Ellie.

"Perhaps he's a spy," whispered Will, and he and Stephen looked at each other hopefully. Both the boys thought it would be a fine thing if the sick lad up-stairs proved to be a British spy.

CHAPTER III

"BARLAY"

"MOTHER! Will likes Stevie's prisoner. He says he does!" declared Ellie a few days after the capture of the young Englishman, who was now able to sit up, and who seemed very grateful for the kindness shown him.

Ellie had just come into the kitchen, after carrying a dish of freshly gathered strawberries to "Barlay," as the boys had decided to call the young man.

"Will has discovered that our visitor can tell him a great deal about silkworms, and you know your brother is very anxious to learn about silk," responded Mrs. Barlow.

"What is a silkworm? Will says it is a sort of caterpillar," said Ellie, looking questioningly at her mother who was busy preparing strawberries to preserve. The careful housewives of Connecticut, in Revolutionary days gathered the wild berries and fruits, which were either dried or preserved for use in the long winter months. Ellie had picked a big basketful of fine strawberries in the lower field that morning, and her mother was now hulling the fragrant berries.

"I'll help hull the strawberries, and you tell me about silkworms," continued the little girl, drawing a chair near to the open doorway where her mother was sitting.

"A silkworm is like a caterpillar. But first of all it is a 'spinner' moth. Your brother can tell you more than I can about it, and very likely this young Englishman knows more than both of us. But I do know that the moth lays the eggs from which the silkworm is hatched. It is a little black worm, covered with long hair, with a shiny nose and sixteen small legs, and its only food seems to be the tender leaf of the mulberry," said Mrs. Barlow.

Ellie looked out through the doorway to where Will's mulberry trees were growing on the sunny slope. How wonderful it would be, she thought, to see silkworms at work.

"I wish Will had some silkworms," she said. "How do the silk worms make silk, mother?"

"They spin it, my dear, in a cocoon. They spin out silken threads, just as a spider sends out its slender lines. The silkworm attaches a thread to some object and spins out a network which is called a cocoon, and which is a firm, continuous thread of silk," explained Mrs. Barlow.

"Why couldn't a little girl raise silkworms and make silk?" Ellie asked; but before her mother could reply Will came into the room.

"You ought to see Barlay in Steve's clothes," he exclaimed laughingly. "He looks funny enough. What do you suppose father means to do with him? He wants to come down-stairs to supper, if you are willing."

"Why, yes, indeed. And we must all be very kind to him," replied his mother.

The strawberries were now ready for the preserve kettle, and while her mother measured out the sugar Ellie went to the pantry and brought out a bowl of yellow corn-meal.

"May I make the johnny-cake for supper, mother?" she asked.

"Yes, my dear. Be sure the water is boiling before you turn it over the meal."

Ellie was always very proud indeed when her mother trusted her to cook some simple dish. Like all girls of that time she was taught that it was necessary to learn to do useful things, and that a little girl who could sew neatly, knit, spin and cook, was sure to grow up an accomplished woman.

When Mr. Barlow and Stephen came in supper was ready, and the golden corn-cake was praised and admired when Ellie set it on the table.

Will helped the young Englishman to his seat at the table, where every one except Stephen made him welcome. Stephen felt that this was no way to treat a prisoner. He wanted to take the Tory to Hartford and see what the American authorities would do with him.

But Barlay seemed so embarrassed and shy that even Stephen was sorry for him before supper was over; and it was Stephen who suggested that the stranger should step out to the porch after supper.

"I hope he means to tell us something about himself," said Mr. Barlow, after the boys had left the room. "I must make some decision about him at once."

After the supper dishes were washed Ellie went out on the porch where her brothers were talking with Barlay. The boys were on the broad lower step of the porch looking up into the clear June sky.

"Yes, that's the Pole Star," she heard the young man say. "You can see that the year around. All the other stars move round it. There's an old rhyme which says:

> " 'He who would scan the figured skies,
>   Its brightest gems to tell,
> Must first direct his mind's eye north
> And learn the 'Bear' stars well.' "

And then he pointed out the constellation of the Great Bear. He went on to say that after he ran away from his regiment he had guided his course as well as possible by the stars.

After the young man had gone to bed Mr. and Mrs. Barlow talked with the boys about what it was best to do in regard with him, and it was Stephen who said: "Why can't he stay here? There's work enough for another boy. He knows a lot about stars, and plants and animals."

"Perhaps he won't want to stay," replied Mr. Barlow, "and, while he seems a friendly lad, we must not forget that he has been an English soldier, and that it is not impossible that he is a spy. The British are in New York, and their ships near our coast. Our Connecticut towns may be attacked at any time. We must be very careful with all strangers, even when they are boys like my namesake."

"Then you think I had better keep watch?" said Stephen.

"Yes, my son. This young fellow is your prisoner, and you are responsible for him. Treat him well, but do not tell him anything of our affairs. When I am called to my regiment do not let him know what it is that takes me from home," said Mr. Barlow.

"But if he doesn't want to stay here, father?" questioned Ellie, clasping her father's arm so tightly that Mr. Barlow realized that his little daughter was alarmed by the talk of spies.

"Yes, we must think of that," he answered; "of course, if he is a spy he will try to steal away without our knowledge. There are Tories in Hartford who would help him along. And that is what Stephen must look out for."

"*I* don't believe he is a spy," declared Will, "and I don't think it would be fair to hand him over to the

American authorities. Of course they'd not believe what he says."

"But he doesn't say anything," Mrs. Barlow reminded him.

"Well, he told me that he thought the Americans were right to defend their homes," confessed Will.

Mr. and Mrs. Barlow decided that the young deserter should be treated in a friendly manner, and asked to help in the work of the farm. "Unless he makes some effort to leave, or deceives us in some way, we will try to make a good American of him," said Mr. Barlow.

"But what could Stevie do if he runs away?" asked Ellie.

"I'll see that he doesn't run away," declared Stephen, feeling that at last he was really in charge of a Tory prisoner. "If I see any signs of it I'll march him straight off to Hartford."

The next day Barlay was down-stairs in good season. He asked Will if there were any pieces of well-seasoned wood to be had, and if Will had a sharp knife. And Will was ready to furnish both, and greatly interested to see what Barlay wanted of them.

"I thought I could make some reels for your mother's yarn," Barlay explained; so Stephen and Will soon followed their father to the field, leaving the young man sitting just outside the kitchen door, pleasantly occupied with his knife.

In response to a sign from Stephen Ellie followed him from the house.

"Look here, Ellie; I want you to keep watch over this fellow until I get back from the field. Mother says he is too weak now even to attempt to get away; but just the same we mustn't take a chance. If he even starts to go toward the road or the woods you blow the horn three times," whispered Stephen.

"Yes, yes, Stevie," Ellie promised, and ran back to the kitchen, resolved to watch the young Englishman as carefully as Stephen would himself.

"May I bring my sewing out here, mother?" she asked, running into the kitchen, where Mrs. Barlow was ironing at a table drawn near the open door.

"Yes, my dear; and you had best take your chair outdoors in the shade beside Barlay, for this room is almost too warm for comfort," replied her mother, and in a few moments Ellie was sitting near the young Englishman, stitching away on the new gingham dress which she was to wear to Hartford.

Barlay had looked up and smiled pleasantly at the little girl, and in a moment Ellie said:

"I am going on a journey in the big coach next Thursday. I am going to Hartford."

"Are you going alone?" asked the English boy.

Ellie nodded proudly. "Yes; but I go straight to my grandmother's," she answered.

Barlay was evidently very clever with his knife. He made a number of fine reels for Mrs. Barlow, and when Stephen came racing across the field in time for dinner his "prisoner" was carving out a tiny box, in the shape of an acorn, as a case for Ellie's thimble.

CHAPTER IV

OFF TO HARTFORD

WILL and Stephen were greatly interested in discovering the names of the stars. And the next evening the family all went to the top of the little hill behind the house, and the young Englishman pointed out two shining stars to the left of the Great Bear.

"Those are Mizar and Alcor," he said. "In olden times the Arabs used these two stars as a test for eyesight, and any Arab who could not see Mizar and Alcor distinctly with his naked eye was not allowed to serve as a soldier."

Each one of the Barlows declared that they could see the stars clearly. Ellie began to wish that she was not going to Hartford quite so soon.

"Will and Stevie will know all about the stars before I get home," she said as her mother went up-stairs with her that night.

"Then they can tell you, dear child," replied Mrs. Barlow, "and I heard Barlay promise Will to make a little chart showing the stars which form the Great Bear, and you will have that to help you. Our visitor is as good as a teacher. But you must remember not to speak of him to any one; not even to grandmother."

"May I wear my shoes with the buckles on my journey?" asked Ellie.

"Why, yes. You will not need your old shoes in Hartford. You can wear the buckled shoes every day; and I will write grandma to buy you some new shoes," said Mrs. Barlow.

The next day Ellie finished her dress, and Mrs. Barlow set the last stitches in the pretty gown of flecked silk. The little leather trunk, which belonged to Ellie's mother, stood in Ellie's room neatly packed for the journey.

"It will be best to put your blue silk hat in my bandbox," said Mrs. Barlow, when she had locked the little trunk. "You can carry the bandbox; then you will be sure that your hat does not get crushed."

"Yes, indeed," agreed Ellie delightedly, feeling that she would really be much more like "Miss Ellen Elizabeth Barlow" if she carried a bandbox.

"So you are going to Hartford to-morrow?" said the young Englishman, when he gave her the pretty carved wooden box for her thimble. "I wonder if you would do an errand there for me?"

"Oh, yes, indeed! and thank you for this fine little box," responded Ellie, looking at the little case with admiring eyes.

Barlay was sitting at the kitchen table with some papers spread out before him. He was making a drawing, or chart, showing the constellation of the Great Bear and the Pole Star. Mrs. Barlow was up-stairs, and for the moment Ellie was alone with the stranger.

"What is the errand?" asked Ellie, remembering that Steve had said that the young Englishman wore a money belt with gold pieces in it, and thinking he probably wanted to send to Hartford for clothing.

"I will tell you just before you start. Please do not speak of it until then," he replied.

Ellie agreed smilingly. She was no longer afraid of Steve's "spy." The Barlow family felt quite sure that there must be some bond of relationship between the young Englishman, whose name was the same as Mr. Barlow's, since Mr. Barlow's father had come to America from the same town where Barlay was born. And, although they were still watchful, they felt very friendly toward the youth.

Thursday morning dawned with clear skies, and with all the beauty and fragrance of a June day. Young robins were hopping about on the newly-cut grass path which led down to the road, and a pleasant little wind from the west brought the fragrance of summer woods and fields.

By ten o'clock Ellie was ready for her journey. The boys had carried the little leather trunk down to the gate; Mrs. Barlow had filled a little basket with a luncheon of cold sliced chicken, bread and butter and a molasses cake; and Ellie had brought her bandbox out to the front porch.

"How long will you stay in Hartford, Miss Ellen?" asked Barlay, who stood just inside the doorway.

"I am to stay a month. Four whole weeks, unless I am homesick," replied Ellie; "but Mr. Pettigrew, the stage-driver, will bring anything you want from Hartford."

Barlay stepped out on the porch, looked sharply about, and in an instant had untied the broad tape with which the bandbox was tied, and had slipped in a small package.

"Do not open your bandbox until you are in your own room at your grandmother's. My errand is written on the paper inside. Don't speak of it to any one. Promise!" he whispered hurriedly. And Ellie, hardly realizing what she said, nodded and agreed.

"Good-bye. When you come back you'll find a surprise; something you will like," said Barlay, and swiftly returned to the kitchen where he was making a fine cupboard for Mrs. Barlow.

For a moment Ellie stood looking at her bandbox, and wondering why Barlay had asked her to keep his errand a secret. But she had little time to think about it, for her father and Steve were coming up from their work in the field to see her safely into the coach; and

Will came running from the shed saying that the coach was in sight. Then Mrs. Barlow, carrying the little lunch basket, came out, and they all walked down the grass path to the road.

Ellie held tight to her father's hand. Suddenly she remembered that he might be called to his regiment any day, and that when she came home he might be far away.

"Be a good and obedient child, Ellie," he said as he gave her a good-bye kiss. And Ellie promised tearfully.

"I would rather stay home with you, father!" she declared.

But Mr. Barlow smiled and said: "Here comes the coach. So remember that you are a brave little Connecticut girl, and don't let Mr. Pettigrew see Miss Ellen Elizabeth Barlow crying."

In a moment, with a great flourish, the big stage-coach with its four brown horses drew up directly in front of the gate, and Ellie's trunk was lifted to the back of the coach, and Ellie and her bandbox were safe inside. There were more good-byes; the stage-driver waved his whip, the horses started, and Ellie, grasping the bandbox with one hand and the lunch basket with the other, was off for the long-hoped-for visit. As she leaned from the coach window and waved her handkerchief to the little group at the gate she forgot all about the joys in store for her. She was going away from home for the first time, and for a moment she was ready to stop the coach and give up the visit. Then she heard a pleasant voice say: "Well, young miss! Off to Hartford, are you?" and she looked around to find herself facing a pleasant elderly lady who sat beside her.

"Yes, ma'am," Ellie replied. "I am going to visit my grandmother."

The old lady laughed and nodded. Her laugh was so pleasant a sound that Ellie wished she might hear it again.

"Then we are really good traveling companions, for I am going to visit my grandchildren," said the old lady. "But I am more fortunate than you are. For you have only one grandmother to see, while I have four little granddaughters."

"Yes, ma'am," Ellie agreed, hoping that the old lady would laugh again. But her companion was opening a fine velvet bag, and in a moment she held out a round box toward Ellie.

"A bit of rock-candy?" she suggested, and Ellie helped herself to a piece, thinking that after all it was a fine thing to go on a journey.

The other passengers were men, evidently tired by their journey. They took no notice of the old lady or of Ellie, who had the back seat to themselves.

"A BIT OF ROCK-CANDY?"

"I've come a long distance, way from Albany," said the old lady. "To be sure, I have stopped over a couple of nights on the way, but 'tis a hard journey."

"Yes, ma'am," Ellie agreed politely, wondering if it would be polite to ask the names of the granddaughters. But she decided that it would not be, for her mother had often cautioned her about asking questions, and told her that whatever people wished her to know they would tell her. So Ellie smiled at her new friend and thanked her for the candy. Then she said:

"My name is Ellen Elizabeth Barlow, but they call me Ellie for a baby name."

"Thank you, my dear. My name is Mrs. Abigail Mason Ludlow, and I am very happy to make your acquaintance," replied Mrs. Ludlow, with a little bow, which Ellie imitated as well as she could.

"And now that we are really acquainted I must ask what you think of His Majesty, the King?" asked Mrs. Ludlow.

"Why, he is not fair to the American Colonies," Ellie replied, repeating what she had so often heard her elders say in so sober a tone that Mrs. Ludlow's eyes seemed to dance, and she nodded approvingly, and again opened her fine bag.

"I can see that you are no Tory child," she said, again holding out the round box. "Have a bit of candy, my dear," and again Ellie helped herself, and thanked Mrs. Ludlow.

The pleasant breeze drifted in through the open windows as the coach dashed along over the country roads. Ellie looked out with delighted eyes at the fields and woodlands, and when the man who always sat on a high seat at the back of the coach, and always jumped down to open the door for passengers, and to help with baggage, blew his long horn as they neared some little settlement or remote farmhouse the little girl smiled happily and thought to herself that it was really a wonderful thing to ride in the big coach. Her bandbox was on the seat beside her, and every now and then she would take hold of the broad tape with which her mother had fastened it.

"You take great care of your bandbox, my dear," said Mrs. Ludlow, and was surprised at Ellie's sudden start.

"I suppose it contains your best hat," she added.

"Yes, ma'am. It is of blue shirred silk," Ellie responded, hoping that Mrs. Ludlow might not ask for a peep at it. For Ellie had suddenly become afraid of the secret which the bandbox held. Suppose, she thought, that Steve's prisoner really was a British spy, and that she was carrying some message for him to the enemies of American freedom? The very thought made the little girl shiver. "I won't take it out of the bandbox at all," she resolved. "Then no harm can be done."

"We will be stopping to change horses soon, I expect," said Mrs. Ludlow, "and I hope I can get a cup of tea."

At this one of the men on the front seat turned, and, taking off his hat, said: "Yes, madam. We are very near the tavern where fresh horses will be put in, and you can get a cup of tea, or an excellent meal. I pass this way often."

"Thank you, sir," replied Mrs. Ludlow.

"I have a luncheon in my basket. There is enough for us both," said Ellie.

"You are very kind, my dear, and I will be happy to share your luncheon. With a cup of good tea I shall be greatly refreshed," responded Ellie's new friend.

In a short time the coach drew up in front of a long brick house near the road. The man on the high seat called out: "Thirty minutes' stop," leaped lightly to the ground and opened the coach door.

The passengers were all eager to get out. Mrs. Ludlow declared that it was the best news she could hear that she could have a cup of tea. At last Ellie was the only one remaining in the coach.

"Come, my child. It will do you good to run about a little. Your journey is not yet half over," said Mrs. Ludlow, and Ellie rather reluctantly followed her, holding the bandbox very carefully.

"You need not take the bandbox, Ellen; it will be quite safe in the coach," said her friend.

"If you please, I think I must take it," Ellie responded, in so serious a tone that Mrs. Ludlow decided that the little girl must be very proud of the blue shirred silk hat.

But Ellie was not thinking of the hat; she was thinking of the little package. If it was some information about Connecticut soldiers for the enemy and if it was found in her bandbox she dared not think what might befall her. She resolved that, no matter what any one might say, she would not let the bandbox out of her sight for a moment.

CHAPTER V

ELLIE HEARS OF A SPY

ELLIE sat down beside Mrs. Ludlow at a long table in the front room of the inn. A pleasant-faced waitress brought her a glass of milk and a cup of tea for Mrs. Ludlow, and they enjoyed the excellent luncheon from Ellie's basket.

The bandbox stood on the floor beside her chair, where she could touch it with her foot, but Ellie was uneasy, and glad when the time came to take her place in the coach. When the fresh horses started off at a fine pace she smiled with such evident satisfaction that Mrs. Ludlow smiled also, and said: "I can see that you will be glad to reach Hartford."

"I have never been on a visit before," said Ellie, "and I have never had any little girl neighbors; and my grandmother has four little girl neighbors who will come and see me."

"Have you no sisters?" questioned Mrs. Ludlow.

Then Ellie told her about Stephen and Will, and how much Steve wanted to be a soldier. But she did not tell of her brother's prisoner. Her mother and father had both cautioned her not to speak of David Barlow to any one. Not even to Grandmother Hinman was she to tell of the deserter, if such he really proved to be.

Now and then some traveler on horseback would pass the coach, and once a number of men rode by at so swift a pace that the passengers in the coach leaned out to look after them, and one of the men in the middle seat said they were American soldiers.

"General Washington has asked for more men," said the man who had told Mrs. Ludlow about the inn, "and these fellows are probably on their way to join the American forces. Connecticut men are always ready," he concluded.

"And are you an American soldier, sir?" asked Mrs. Ludlow.

"I have that honor, madam," replied the young man smilingly; "but just now I am on special service. I am on the outlook for a young English spy who is reported to be at work near Hartford."

As Ellie heard this she nearly fell from her seat, and she looked at the young American with such an expression of terror that he could not but notice it, and he smiled and nodded in a friendly manner.

"Do not be afraid, little maid. An English spy is not greatly to be feared, and I shall soon have him safe."

"Is—is—is the spy an old man?" questioned Ellie.

"Why, no. The fellow I am after is not much more than a lad, but a very clever lad," replied the man.

Ellie was sure now that Steve's suspicion of his prisoner had been right. It was all too dreadful, she thought. Here she was journeying to Hartford and carrying a message for the enemy of America in her fine bandbox.

"Oh! I must go home! I must!" she cried, in so unhappy a tone that all the passengers turned to look at her.

"Why, is the child frightened at the very name of an English soldier?" asked the young man. "I am sorry I spoke."

"'Tis her first absence from home," replied Mrs. Ludlow, putting her arm about Ellie; "she will soon smile again. You will be in Hartford in an hour or so, my dear; quite safe with your grandmother," she said.

"I'm not afraid," declared Ellie, "but the spy—"

The young man looked at her sharply, but when Ellie added, "I want to tell my father," he smiled again.

"Oh, your father will know a spy when he sees him, never fear," he said reassuringly. But Ellie was very quiet all the rest of the journey. She sat very close to Mrs. Ludlow, and as they now passed through villages and came nearer to the town of Hartford Mrs. Ludlow would point out some place of interest to the little girl, endeavoring to make her forget the English spy.

"I suppose you know all about the Charter Oak, do you not?" questioned Mrs. Ludlow, and when Ellie shook her head, Mrs. Ludlow seemed greatly surprised.

"Why, 'tis as fine a story as you could wish to hear," she declared, "and the old charter was a pattern for an American Commonwealth. You must see the oak; 'tis not too far to visit. Why, I will take you myself, since we are both to be visitors in Hartford. Now, where does your grandmother live?"

"In Market Square," Ellie replied. "The stage-driver is to leave me at her house."

"Well, well! And my daughter's house is in Market Square also. We will be neighbors, and I will surely set a day to visit the Charter Oak with you," said Mrs. Ludlow, and for a moment Ellie forgot the spy. She recalled that Mrs. Ludlow had said that she had four little granddaughters. Perhaps they were the little Chaplin girls. She was quite sure that it would not be impolite to ask.

"If you please, are your little granddaughters' names Bertha and Mildred and Nancy and Lucy?" she asked.

"Why, yes, indeed!" replied Mrs. Ludlow, with the laugh which Ellie thought so delightful, "and are they your grandmother's neighbors? Now, we will all have a beautiful visit together. Why, we could not have planned anything better than this if we had known each other for years."

Ellie smiled happily. It was surely a happy chance that had given her Mrs. Ludlow for a traveling companion, and the kindly old lady began to tell her about

Bertha and Mildred, both of whom had visited her in Albany in the previous summer. She said that Bertha must be taller than Ellie. "And she is old for her years, a very thoughtful, useful girl," declared the proud grandmother. "I know your Grandmother Hinman very well, my dear, and she has been a kind friend and neighbor to my daughter."

"Would you tell me the story about the Charter Oak?" asked Ellie, feeling sure that the little Chaplin girls must know all about it, and if they should ask her about it and she did not know she would feel that Bertha and Mildred might think her an ignorant girl.

"Yes, my dear; I will tell you to the best of my ability."

The young American soldier turned about and was evidently desirous of hearing the story.

"Of course you know that Hartford was a fine town a hundred years ago? Yes, indeed. And the people of Connecticut had a charter, that is, an agreement signed by King Charles II, giving them the rights of free and independent men. Well, when a new king came to England's throne he decided that he would take away this charter, and in 1687 he sent Sir Edward Andros to take the charter. The fine Englishman arrived in Hartford; the charter was brought to him at twilight, and as it lay on the table before him—out went the candles—there was a rustling of paper, and when the candles were relighted the charter was gone. But every one was in the room!

"Well, of course there was a great search! But it was not found. No indeed! It had been slipped through the window to young Wadsworth, who was off and away with it to the house of Farmer Wyllis, where the paper was safely hidden in a cavity in the old oak. And it was in that manner that it was kept from English hands."

Ellie gave a long breath of satisfaction, and the young man nodded approvingly. "The tree has another story as well as the hiding of the charter," he said. "It was planted by an Indian sachem as a pledge of perpetual peace with the people of Connecticut, and the Indians buried their tomahawks under it."

"Shall we go to see the tree very soon?" Ellie questioned, quite forgetting her resolve to return home on the very next day, even if she had to walk all the distance.

"Just as soon as possible, my dear. Perhaps we shall have a picnic, my little granddaughters, your grandmother, and you and I," replied Mrs. Ludlow.

And now the coach had really entered Hartford. The guard's bugle calls sounded louder, the horses seemed to go faster, and the driver's whip was flourished in wonderful sweeps as they rounded corners, drove past shops and houses and finally drew up before the door of a fine brick mansion-house. In an instant the coach door swung open, the steps were lowered, and Ellie was at her journey's end. Grandmother Hinman was coming down the little path to the street to welcome her, and two little girls came running toward the coach, calling out: "Grandma Ludlow! Grandma Ludlow!" So that in a moment after her grandmother's greeting Ellie found herself smiling up at a tall girl whose eyes were exactly like Mrs. Ludlow's, and heard her grandmother say:

"Bertha, this is my little granddaughter, Ellen. I hope you will be fast friends."

The tall girl smiled soberly and held out her hand. "How do you do?" she said. "This is my sister Mildred," and Mildred nodded and bowed, but did not seem to notice that Ellen expected to shake hands.

Then with good-nights the little group separated, and Grandmother Hinman led Ellie into the big hall and up the broad stairs to a square room at the back of the house, the windows of which overlooked the most beautiful garden that the little girl had ever seen.

"Oh, grandma! I meant to bring you some of my yellow roses, and I forgot all about it!" exclaimed Ellie, as she noticed a blue bowl filled with yellow roses on a table in the corner of the room.

"Well, dear child, I am more pleased to see you than any rose you could bring," responded grandmother. "This room was your mother's room, my dear. And this bedspread is one she knit when she was no older than you are," and Mrs. Hinman touched the snowy cover of the bed, with its four tall slender posts.

"Here is Hannah Jane," continued grandma when, after a loud rap on the door, it swung open and a tall woman with wide shoulders, and looking very stern and silent, came into the room.

"This is Ellen, Hannah Jane," said grandma; and the big woman set down the pitcher of hot water, and nodded severely.

"I trust your mither and fa-a-ther are well, Miss Ellen," she said.

"Yes, thank you," Ellen responded, rather faintly, for she felt a little afraid of this stern person, "and my mother sent her love to you," she added.

At this a broad smile crept over the woman's face.

"Did she now? Weel! 'Tis herself that was always the best of young ladies. An' I have small doubt but that you'll do her credit," she said, nodding pleasantly.

Then she stalked out of the room, and in a moment Grandma Hinman followed, saying: "Come right down to the dining-room, dear. Hannah Jane's hot biscuit will be cooling."

"I must ask her to tell me about the Scotch rose," thought Ellie, as she filled the big basin with warm water and began bathing her hands and face.

"Oh!" she exclaimed suddenly, looking about the room. "Where is my bandbox?"

She ran about looking in every part of the chamber, and opened the closet door. But the bandbox was not to be found. Peter, the man who took care of the garden, cleaned windows, and tended fires, had brought up the little leather trunk, which grandma had said they would unpack after supper, but there was no bandbox to be seen.

CHAPTER VI

THE SCOTCH ROSE

"OH! What can I do! What can I do!" Ellie exclaimed aloud, as she searched the room for the missing box. For she had now convinced herself that Barlay's errand was surely some dangerous message for the enemies of American freedom, and she quite forgot all her delight in the beautiful garden she had seen from her chamber windows, and the joys in store for her in the friendship of the little Chaplin girls.

She heard the sound of a tinkling bell, but did not understand that it was a call to supper until Grandmother Hinman opened the door.

"Why, my dear child, surely you are not homesick?" she exclaimed, noticing Ellie's tear-stained cheeks and her unhappy expression.

"No, grandma," said Ellie, choking back a sob, but not daring to speak of the lost bandbox. Some way, she resolved, she must recover the bandbox without any one knowing of how careless she had been. So she went down to supper. But she hardly noticed the fine silver dishes on the table, or the candlesticks which shone so brightly on the tall mantelpiece. She had so little appetite for the hot biscuit and broiled trout, or for the square of rich cake, that Mrs. Hinman and Hannah Jane exchanged anxious looks over their little visitor.

"I think you are tired, and must go early to bed, my dear," grandmother said as they left the dining-room together. Before Ellie could respond there sounded a loud knock at the front door, and Ellie heard a gruff voice saying something in regard to a bandbox.

"Oh! It's my bandbox!" she exclaimed, running toward the hall, and meeting Hannah Jane who was coming toward them carrying the box.

"I forgot it. I left it in the coach," exclaimed Ellie.

"Weel, weel! The man as fetched it said he wondered at ye forgettin' it, since ye hardly let go of it for the journey," said Hannah Jane.

"I don't know how I could have forgotten it," said Ellie very soberly. "It is my fine shirred hat of blue silk," she explained, and she picked up the treasured box with such an expression of satisfaction that her grandmother and Hannah Jane both smiled.

Ellie was so rejoiced to have the bandbox safe and sound that she quite forgot to worry about the contents, and ran up-stairs talking happily to Grandma Hinman, and telling her all the messages her mother had sent.

"And mother will send me a letter by the coach next Thursday; and I am to send her a letter by Mr. Pettigrew. I will have a great deal to tell her," she said, thinking of Mrs. Ludlow, the little Chaplin girls, and her grandmother's fine garden.

"Will you tell me the story of your yellow rose-tree to-morrow, grandma?" she asked, as Grandmother Hinman helped her unpack the little trunk and hung the pretty silk dress in the closet.

"Yes, indeed; 'tis a story which I have told your mother many times," replied Mrs. Hinman, "and when we go out to the garden to-morrow morning you shall hear all about Queen Mary's rose."

"But I thought it was a Scotch rose?" said Ellie.

"So it is, my dear. But Scotland's queen brought it from France for her garden at Holyrood."

"Oh, grandma! From France! Every time I ask about my rose I hear something new. My rose came from your garden, and your rose came from Holyrood, and the rose-tree there came from France! Why, it must be a wonderful story," said Ellie, hoping that her grandmother would tell her the story that very night.

But Mrs. Hinman smiled and nodded, and said that it was a wonderful story, and that Ellie should hear it the very next day. "But now, my dear, you must say your prayers and go to sleep, for you must be tired," she concluded, leaning over to give Ellie her good-night kiss, and a moment later Ellie was in the big bed thinking of all the good times which were sure to begin the next morning. She began to say over the story of her yellow rose: "My garden, grandma's garden, Holyrood garden, France—" but her eyes closed and she was off to dreamland, to sleep soundly until the morning sun came streaming into the chamber.

For a moment Ellie looked around the room with wondering eyes. She thought she must still be asleep. Then she exclaimed aloud, sitting up in bed: "Oh! This is my grandmother's; I am on a visit to Hartford!"

"Yes, indeed!" responded grandma, who had just entered the room, "and Bertha and Mildred Chaplin have come in to take breakfast with us; and there are strawberries and griddle-cakes for breakfast."

Ellie hastened to dress, and to brush out her dark curls and tie them back with a narrow crimson ribbon which Grandmother Hinman gave her. She put on a dress of white linen which her mother had woven and made for her, and white stockings which she had knit herself, and when she was quite ready her grandmother looked at her with approving eyes.

"I hope the little Chaplin girls will like me, grandmother," Ellie whispered as they went down the wide stairs.

"Of course they will, my dear child; of course they will," replied Mrs. Hinman, quite sure that no one could help liking her dark-eyed little granddaughter.

The dining-room seemed full of sunshine. It came in through the two open windows, and danced across the polished floor, glimmering on the white table-cloth and the tall pewter pitcher, and shining back from the mirror over the high mantel. As Ellie came into the room and Bertha and Mildred turned from one of the windows where they were standing, she thought that their hair was exactly like sunlight—it was so yellow and shining.

The two sisters smiled and said good-morning in such friendly tones that Ellie felt that the good times had already begun.

Bertha said that Mrs. Ludlow sent her love, and hoped that Ellie would soon come and see her. As soon as breakfast was over Grandma Hinman led the way to the garden. A door from the dining-room opened directly on a terrace where mignonette, larkspurs, columbines, and clumps of iris grew. Two or three steps led from the terrace to the rose-garden, where, over a rustic summer-house, climbed the yellow rose-tree. There were many other roses, white and crimson, and a delicate pink. All around the garden were shrubs, and a high hedge of prickly thorn. There was an opening in this hedge which led into a prosperous vegetable garden, where potatoes, cabbages, beets, turnips and carrots and many other vegetables grew; and where Peter, Hannah Jane's brother, was now at work.

"The summer-house is always pleasant in the morning," said Grandmother Hinman, "and the yellow rose is now in full bloom. You can see how well it has liked its home," and she pointed to the stout trunk of the rose-tree, from which many sturdy branches grew.

There was a broad, comfortable seat built all around the inside of the arbor, and here the little party sat down. Grandma took out from the bag which she carried the yarn sock she was knitting; and Bertha and Mildred, from a deep pocket in the apron they each wore, also drew out their shining needles and balls of gray yarn. For the soldiers of the American army depended on the women of the country for their supply of clothing, and there were few idle hands in city or country.

"I have not any work!" said Ellie, ashamed to sit idle when the others were so busily occupied.

"I will take up a stocking for you this afternoon," replied grandma, "but this morning it will do no harm for you to be idle."

"Was Queen Mary a little girl when she planted her rose-bush?" asked Mildred.

"Not when she planted the rose-tree at Holyrood. She was a fine young lady then, who had just safely returned from France," replied grandmother.

"You see, Mary Stuart's mother wanted her little daughter to grow up in France, thinking that she would have greater advantages there than in Scotland; so when Mary was about six years old she was taken to the court of the King of France where she was warmly received.

"Now, when little Mary Stuart went to France a party of friends went with her; and there were four other little girls in the party. And every one of these four was named Mary."

Bertha and Ellie smiled at each other. A story about five little girls all with the same name was sure to be a fine story, they thought.

"Well," continued grandma, "the young Queen Mary was very fond of garden work, and in her own garden at St. Germain was a rose-bush with so many little yellow roses that she declared it was the loveliest rose in all the garden. So the other little girls began calling it 'Queen Mary's Rose.' But the servants of the household and her friends called it the 'Scotch Rose,' because Mary was Queen of Scotland. And Queen Mary herself began to call it the Scotch Rose.

"When she grew up into young womanhood and married a French prince and on his death decided to return to her own country, she said to her four Marys that she must take her Scotch rose to Edinburgh; and the story is that her friends had the rose-tree carefully dug up with a great deal of earth, and that it was cared for tenderly on the journey and set out in a sunny corner of the garden of Holyrood; and the gardener there gave my father the little slip from which this very rose-tree grew," concluded grandmother, pointing a knitting needle toward the beautiful yellow roses which nodded over the arbor.

"Oh!" exclaimed Mildred, drawing a long breath, "I think that is a fine story. I like true stories."

"So do I," declared both the other girls.

"I wish our names were all the same," said Bertha thoughtfully.

Grandmother Hinman said that she would now have to return to the house, but that the girls could stay in the arbor, or walk about in the garden; and she left the little girls to make friends.

Mrs. Hinman had hardly left the arbor when Bertha jumped up and said: "I've thought of a lovely plan. With Nancy and Lucy and we three there are five little girls, just as there were with Queen Mary."

"But our names are not the same," objected Mildred.

"Wait, Mildred! I suppose our names could be all the same, couldn't they? I don't mean 'Mary.' But we can think of some fine name and then we can call each other by it, but not before other people," replied Bertha, slipping her knitting into her apron pocket.

"Then it is to be a secret?" asked Ellie, her eyes shining with delight; for to have a secret with four other girls seemed to her as wonderful as the story of the Scotch rose.

"We could all be Rose," she suggested.

"So we could! That is splendid. Then if we forgot and said 'Rose' before other people, they wouldn't think it strange," agreed Bertha. "But as it will be our secret society we must meet this afternoon and plan what we'll do, and take vows."

"What are 'vows'?" asked Ellie.

"A vow is a solemn promise. And we will have to be sure it is solemn if we want Nancy and Lucy not to tell," replied Bertha.

CHAPTER VII

FORT DANGER

IT was agreed that Ellie should go over to the Chaplin house that afternoon to become acquainted with Nancy and Lucy, the two younger girls, and to pay her respects to Mrs. Ludlow. Mrs. Hinman was greatly pleased that her little granddaughter should be so ready to make friends with the Chaplin girls, and Hannah Jane went with Ellie to Mrs. Chaplin's door.

Mrs. Ludlow was sitting on the porch and greeted Ellie warmly.

"And where is the bandbox?" she asked laughingly, but was sorry for her question when she saw how sober the little girl became. For Ellie had not thought of the secret packet, and now she at once remembered all that it might mean. Before she could answer two little girls came running out on the porch and stood beside Mrs. Ludlow's chair, looking shyly toward Ellie. They both had brown curls and brown eyes, and although Nancy was eight and Lucy only six they were very nearly of a size.

"Nancy and Lucy, this is my friend Miss Ellen Barlow," said Mrs. Ludlow, and Nancy and Lucy both curtsied very prettily, and smiled shyly at the older girl.

Before these greetings were over Bertha and Mildred appeared and suggested that Ellie should go into the garden with them.

"'Tis not so fine a garden as Madame Hinman's, but 'tis a fine place to play," said Bertha, leading the way down the path and around to the back of the house. There was no terrace or arbor in the Chaplin garden, but there were a number of fine cherry trees, now covered with nearly ripened fruit. There were several tall elms whose spreading branches made a pleasant shade in one corner of the enclosure, many blossoming shrubs, and here and there beds of peonies, columbine and sweet-scented herbs.

The garden was enclosed by a brick wall, and just beyond the elm trees a gate opened into a field which sloped down to the river. Bertha led the way across the garden, and opened the gate, and waited until the others had passed through, then she closed the gate and latched it carefully.

"There are cows in this field, and we are always careful to fasten the gate," she explained to Ellie, "so they won't get into the garden."

Mildred and Lucy ran on ahead toward the river, and Nancy, who kept very close to Ellie, cried eagerly:

"Shall we go in wading, Bertha? There's a lovely place," she continued, turning to Ellie, "a shady cove. Mother lets us go wading nearly every day."

"We must not go wading to-day. We did not ask permission," replied Bertha soberly.

Nancy seemed quite sure that whatever Bertha said must be right, and nothing more was said just then about wading.

"Nancy, we have something very serious to tell you and Lucy," continued Bertha as they walked on. "It's something you can never tell unless Ellen, Mildred, Lucy and I all agree to let you."

"I won't tell!" Nancy promised eagerly. "What is it, Bertha?"

"Wait until we get to the fort, and I will tell you," replied Bertha.

Ellie wondered if they were going to a real fort, but she did not ask. She was soon to discover that Bertha loved everything that had to do with brave deeds, and that her new playmate knew no end of wonderful stories. She had already warned Ellie not to touch the toadstools. "If you do the fairies won't like you," she had explained, "because fairies dance on the toadstools!"

They soon crossed the field and reached the bank of the river where Mildred and Lucy were waiting. The bank shelved steeply down to the water, and there were clumps of meadowsweet growing all along the slope. About halfway down the bank there was a little shelf, or natural platform.

"That is the fort," said Bertha, pointing to it. "We call it Fort Danger, because, you see, it is dangerous to get down there, and dangerous to get back."

"How do you get down?" Ellie questioned a little fearfully.

"Oh, we slide down. Like this," said Mildred, stepping one foot carefully over the edge, sitting down on the slippery grass, which she clutched now and then in order not to go too rapidly.

"That's the way," she called, as she landed safely and looked up at the others. "You come next, Ellie."

It seemed a dangerous adventure to Ellie as she stood looking down the steep slope. Suppose she did not stop on the shelf but went straight over, splash into the river.

"Don't be afraid. Why, even Lucy isn't afraid, and she is only six years old," called Mildred.

"I'm not afraid," Ellie replied, and following Mildred's example she was quickly standing beside Mildred; and in a few moments all five of the little girls stood on the terrace-like projection.

"How do we get back?" asked Ellie, looking up at the steep slippery bank down which she had slid so quickly.

"We can't get back that way," explained Bertha. "We have to go down and take the river path which runs along the edge of the field."

There were piles of small stones heaped up on the edge of the terrace. The Chaplin girls explained that these were "munition," to fire at the enemy.

"What enemy?" questioned Ellie.

"Oh, we make believe that we are early settlers, and that the Indians come and try to drive us away. Don't you ever play make-believe games?" replied Mildred.

Ellie shook her head. "No; you see, I've never had anybody to play with," she said, "but I think 'make-believe' must be splendid."

"Yes; we have lots of 'make-believes,'" said Bertha. "That's why I thought about five of us all having one name."

"Is that the secret, Bertha?" asked Nancy.

"Part of it. You see, Nancy, once there was a queen in Scotland, a little girl queen. And her name was Mary, and there were four other little girls who were her playmates and each one of these little girls was also named 'Mary.' So when Mrs. Hinman told us about them I thought right off that we five could all make believe that our names were all alike," said Bertha.

"Names all alike," repeated Lucy, who was not always included in the games of the older girls, and was now overjoyed to find that she was not to be left out.

"Ellen thinks that 'Rose' would be a good name," continued Bertha, "and I think so, too."

"What else?" questioned Lucy.

"Well, of course, we must begin by always wearing a rose," answered Bertha. "I don't mean a real rose, but we can make some tiny roses out of pieces of silk and wear those. Of course none of us can be a queen, because it's kings and queens who make so much trouble for America. But we must make vows to each other."

"What about?" questioned Mildred.

"We, five Roses, vow solemnly to stand by each other in all true deeds, and to keep this meeting a secret pact," said Bertha. "I don't know what 'pact' means, but it's in one of father's books, so it's all right."

Ellie looked at her new friend admiringly. It seemed to her that Bertha was the most wonderful girl in all the world.

"Now all hold up your right hands and repeat it after me," said Bertha, and with great solemnity the five little girls repeated the vow declaring themselves five Roses. Ellie wondered just what Bertha meant by "true deeds," and when they were all comfortably seated on the soft grass she said:

"What is a 'true deed,' Bertha?"

Bertha's eyes shone just as Ellie remembered Mrs. Ludlow's had done when she had spoken of American soldiers, and she answered quickly:

"A true deed is something splendid; like doing some brave act to help America; or saving somebody's life.

Of course girls don't have as many chances to do brave deeds as boys do," she concluded a little mournfully.

"Would finding a spy be a brave deed?" asked Ellie.

"Why, yes," said Bertha. "It would if you captured him yourself, and delivered him to justice."

Ellie wished that she could tell Bertha about Barlay, and ask her what it was best to do about the package in the flowered bandbox. But she remembered that her mother and father had cautioned her not to speak of the young Englishman to any one.

While Bertha and Ellie were talking the other girls had left the "fort" by sliding down the slope to the river path, and now called up for Bertha and Ellie to join them.

This slide was even more steep than the other, and Ellie was glad when Nancy said: "We come to Fort Danger only when we have secrets to tell, or something serious to plan." To Ellie it seemed a "brave deed" to reach the fort, and a very difficult thing to get away.

Near the foot of the bluff was a sandy beach, over-hung by the branches of a tall elm tree.

"There is where we go in wading," said Mildred, pointing toward the little cove. "I wish we had asked permission to go in today. It is so warm."

The girls were standing on a grassy bank at the edge of the stream. Ellie was nearest to the water, and suddenly she felt the grass yield beneath her feet, and at the same instant heard Mildred call: "Don't step there, Ellen!"

But the warning came too late. She had stepped on some long grass which overhung the bank, and had fallen into the river. She was absolutely helpless, and every effort that she made to regain the shore sent her farther out into deeper water. She was thoroughly frightened, and when the water swept her entirely off her feet she called out wildly. At that moment she was seized by each arm, and half led, half carried to shore.

CHAPTER VIII

THE PACKAGE VANISHES

WHEN Bertha and Mildred realized that Ellie could not help herself in her efforts to reach the shore they had both waded into the water to her assistance. And now three very wet and bedraggled little girls stood on the shore, while Nancy and Lucy, frightened and silent, stood looking at them.

Ellie's hat had drifted off beyond reach. Her hair hung over her face, her buckled shoes were spoiled, and her white stockings and dress covered with mud. Bertha and Mildred were splashed and dripping, but were not in nearly so bad a condition as their new friend.

"I'm drowned!" sobbed Ellie. "I fell in and drowned."

"We must hurry home as fast as we can," said Bertha, who had knelt down beside Ellie and was trying to wring some of the water from Ellie's skirt. "Don't cry, Ellen. It was all our fault. We ought to have told you not to go so near the river."

Ellie's sobs ceased quickly. "I never fell in a river before," she said, as if to explain her fright. "I think you were both brave to come in after me."

72

"Oh, we can both swim. And even if we had not been able to swim, of course we would have come and helped you," said Bertha, as they made their way along the river path toward home.

At every step Ellie could hear the "slush, slush" of the water in her fine shoes, of which she had always been so careful.

"I think it was a 'true deed' for you to wade right out into that wide river," persisted Ellie, "and you kept the vow: 'to stand by each other in all true deeds.'"

"So we did!" exclaimed Mildred, "but I never thought about the vow."

Nancy and Lucy had run on ahead, and when the other three girls reached the gate which led into the garden Mrs. Ludlow and Mrs. Chaplin were running across the garden toward them.

"I fell in the river and drowned," Ellie explained cheerfully, being quite sure that a thorough drenching and being drowned must be the same. "And Bertha and Mildred did a true deed and brought me out," she added.

"I will step over to Mrs. Hinman's with Ellen, and explain to her," suggested Mrs. Ludlow, while Mrs. Chaplin hurried Bertha and Mildred up-stairs to put on dry clothing.

The fact that the "Five Roses" had lived up to their secret vow was a great comfort to the girls. Ellie wished that Mrs. Ludlow could know all about it, but she was glad enough to slip out of her wet clothes and to have Hannah Jane rub her feet and help her into a fresh dress.

"But I haven't any other shoes," she exclaimed, as she sat on the little footstool. "And I have lost my hat."

"Dinna cry about it," said Hannah Jane sharply. "There's many a poor child without a pair of shoes or a hat to its feet. I'll step over to Mistress Chaplin's and borrow a pair of slippers, and to-morrow your grandmother will be buying you what you need," and Hannah Jane stalked out of the room carrying the wet shoes and the dripping clothing.

As Ellie sat there in the pleasant chamber waiting for Hannah Jane's return she repeated over to herself, "There's many a poor child without a pair of shoes or a hat to its feet," at first with a little giggle of amusement at Hannah Jane's manner of speech, and then with a wonder if there really were little girls who went without shoes and hats. She resolved to ask Hannah Jane if she knew any such little girls.

"Here's some fine slippers," said Hannah Jane. "They belong to Miss Bertha, but you are to wear them and welcome."

"Are there little girls who never have shoes and hats?" Ellie asked soberly, as she followed the tall Scotchwoman from the room.

"To be sure there are such children," Hannah Jane answered, "and it becomes a young lady to think of them, and not of her own lacks."

Ellie was eager to explain that she had never known there were such children; but at that moment her grandmother appeared at the foot of the stairs, and in answering her questions about the accident Ellie forgot about the children of whom Hannah Jane had told her.

"We must go shopping early on Monday morning," said Mrs. Hinman smilingly, as if it was a pleasant task she was considering. "You have your fine blue silk hat, of which you told me, to wear to church to-morrow; so we will not worry about the lost hat and spoiled shoes. And now you had best lie down on the sofa until supper time and rest."

Ellie was quite ready to do this. The big sofa which stood near the western windows of the cool sitting-room was a very pleasant place to rest, and with Grandma Hinman sitting near by at one of the open windows Ellie was well content to curl up with her head on one of the big soft cushions. But as she looked toward her grandmother she realized that Mrs. Hinman was looking out toward the Square, and there was the sound of marching feet passing the house.

In an instant Ellie had sprung from the sofa and run across the room.

"What is it, grandma?" she asked eagerly, looking out at a line of soldiers going by to the music of fife and drum.

"It must be that General Washington has need of more men in New York; and Connecticut men are ready whenever the call comes to defend their country," replied Mrs. Hinman.

"Will the enemy come to Hartford?" Ellie asked, as the music grew fainter, and the soldiers vanished from sight.

Grandma shook her head. "Who can tell?" she answered. "So far we have had no fear. But there are rumors of spies; and where spies appear there is always trouble at hand."

"Oh-h!" exclaimed Ellie, in so sorrowful and frightened a voice that Grandmother Hinman looked at her in surprise, and put her arm about the little girl.

"Do not be frightened, dear child. We know there is no spy near us," she said.

"What would you do if you found a spy, grandma?" Ellie asked so earnestly that Mrs. Hinman smiled.

"Why, it would depend on circumstances, my dear. If a spy got into my house by deceiving me I should hand him over to the authorities very quickly. It is the first duty of Americans to see that spies are punished," she replied.

"Would it be like a spy to pretend he was sick and had deserted from the British army?" questioned Ellie.

"It is very likely that a spy might do exactly that. But we will not welcome any deserter, dear, so do not look so troubled," said grandma. But Ellie was very quiet and sober during supper, and was glad when the time came for her to go up-stairs to bed.

She opened the closet door and peered in at the big bandbox.

"Oh, dear," she whispered, "I wish I could go right home and let father open that package; then he would know just what to do. Perhaps I ought to tell grandma about it. Perhaps I ought not to keep a promise to a spy." But then she remembered that her mother and father had seemed to trust Barlay, and perhaps, after all, he might not be as wicked as she thought. But the secret packet troubled her, and she dreaded the time when she must take out her silk hat and see Barlay's package in the bandbox.

Ellie slept late the next morning and awoke to find her grandmother standing beside the bed smiling down at her.

"'Tis the Sabbath day, dear child, and we will go to church directly after breakfast. You shall wear your pretty flecked silk, and your fine hat. And the little Chaplin girls will take you to Sunday-school," said grandma.

Ellie smiled happily. To have four little girls waiting to walk to church with her made her quite forget every troublesome and unhappy thought, and she was soon ready for breakfast.

"Now run up and put on the pretty hat," said grandmother, as they left the dining-room.

At the mention of the hat, Ellie's face grew sober. She dreaded to even touch Barlay's packet. But she ran upstairs, lifted the bandbox from its shelf in the closet, untied the tape and lifted the cover. She could not help admiring her pretty hat as she took it from the box. Then she quickly put on the cover, and hurried down the stairs where grandma was waiting.

"It is indeed a pretty hat, and does great credit to your dear mother," said grandma, "and now think no more of fine raiment, but walk soberly."

The little Chaplin girls with their mother and father and Mrs. Ludlow walked along with Mrs. Hinman and Ellie. The little girls smiled at each other, but there was no conversation until after church, and then only a few words of greeting. But Ellie was very happy to know that her new friends were so near to her, and that she and Bertha would walk home together. Now and then she thought of the package, but she had resolved not to be afraid of it. So long as it remained safely in the bandbox it could do no harm.

On returning from church Ellie ran happily up-stairs to put her hat back in the box. She took it off carefully, and put it on a chair, then she opened the box, and for a moment stood staring into it. The box was empty. There was no letter, no package. Nothing. Barlay's message had disappeared.

CHAPTER IX

A DAY OF TROUBLE

ELLIE stood looking into the empty box as if she could hardly believe her own eyes. Her first feeling was one of delight that the packet had vanished. But then came a sudden fear. If Barlay really was a spy perhaps the lost message had already reached the person to whom it was addressed, and how could she know that it had not contained directions to destroy her own home, to take her father a prisoner?

Quite forgetting her blue hat Ellie sat down in the chair facing the open closet and began to cry. But she sprang up suddenly. She had sat down on her hat. There it lay crushed out of shape. She picked it up and began to push it carefully here and there, but still it did not look right, and she decided to tell her grandmother that she had sat down on it, and on the following morning ask her to fix it. The hat seemed of very little importance just then.

Ellie went to the window and looked out over the beautiful garden. Grandma was taking a little rest in her own room, and Hannah Jane and Peter had not yet returned from church. Everything seemed very quiet and peaceful as she tiptoed down the stairs and through the empty house to the garden. She wandered about looking at the flowers, and thinking of the "Five Roses," and of the lost package, and soon found herself at the entrance to the vegetable garden, and walked on toward the far end, where the big red strawberries grew.

There was something queer about the strawberry bed to-day, thought Ellie. What was that queer looking brown object at the further side of the bed? She stood quite still watching it. "It's a girl! A little girl! And she is eating grandmother's strawberries," she whispered to herself, and at that moment the little trespasser turned about and saw Ellie looking at her. For a moment the two children eyed each other. The strange child was bareheaded. Her hair was a dull brown, and hardly darker than her swarthy skin, her eyes were brown, and the little claw-like hands were brown. She stood up quickly, and Ellie noticed that the straight shapeless dress was brown. The child was so small that Ellie thought she could not be more than five or six years old. She was bareheaded and barefooted.

As Ellie looked at her both the little brown hands covered the brown face and the child began to cry.

"Don't cry," Ellie exclaimed, realizing that this must be one of the children that Hannah Jane had said it

SHE TIPTOED DOWN THE STAIRS

would "become" her to think of. "Come over here and tell me who you are."

The child peered at her through her fingers.

"What you going to do to me?" she asked in a shrill little voice. "Be you going to tell your folks you caught me stealing?"

Ellie shook her head. "No, I won't tell. I'm sure my grandma would wish you to have the berries if you are hungry."

"Hungry! Well, I never had enough to eat. I'm always hungry, and so's Joe. See!" and she held up a queer little basket made of leaves and sticks, and nearly filled with fine berries. "I was picking these for Joe."

Ellie nodded approvingly. She did not know that Grandma Hinman set great store by her fine berries, and that on Monday she meant to send a fine basketful as a gift to the wife of her pastor. The strawberries grew wild in the fields all about Ellie's home, and she saw no harm in this brown little girl taking home all the berries she could pick to "Joe," whoever he might be.

"Who is Joe?" she asked.

"He's my brother. He's younger than me," explained the child. "We lives in Brown Lane down near the river. Me father's lame."

"I'll help you pick," declared Ellie, forgetting her fine silk dress, and thinking only of this thin frightened child who stared at her in amazement.

"I never stealed anything before," whimpered the little girl, "an' I hated to sneak into this pretty place, but father's gone off an' Joe and I was hungry."

"Where's your mother?" asked Ellie.

The little girl shook her head. "Guess we never had a mother. Leastways I don't recall her," she answered.

For a moment or two the little girls were silent, each selecting the finest of the berries for "Joe's" basket.

"There! It's full. I guess I ain't stole nothin', so long as you've helped me," said the girl.

"Of course you haven't!" Ellie assured her eagerly. "And if you'll come up to-morrow I'll bring you out some things to eat. What's your name?"

Before the child could answer Ellie heard Hannah Jane calling, and turned to answer. When she again looked for the little brown figure it had vanished. Ellie looked about the garden with anxious eyes.

"And what may you be doing in your grandma's strawberry bed on the Sabbath day, Miss Ellen?" and Ellie turned to find Hannah Jane close beside her, looking very stern and disapproving.

"Did ye not know that your grandma lets no person save Peter an' meself set foot in that bed?" she continued. "A rare mess you've made of it!" and Hannah Jane looked where the girls had ruthlessly pulled the strawberries from the sheltering leaves.

"An' if ye're not sick from it 'twill be little less than a miracle. A full quart of fine berries ye must have eaten! An' on the Sabbath day! Weel! Weel!" and Hannah Jane looked at Ellie accusingly.

"Can ye no speak and say how sorry ye feel?" she questioned reprovingly.

Ellie made no answer. She turned sharply 'round and walked toward the house, angry and ashamed, but not at all sorry. Hannah Jane might say what she pleased, but Ellie resolved that she would not put the blame on the poor half-starved child whom she had discovered in the garden. No hats and no shoes! Well, Hannah Jane could talk finely about hats and shoes; but what about hungry children? thought Ellie as she marched into the house and up to her own chamber.

"I wish I was home," she whispered to herself. "Hannah Jane will tell grandma that I ate a quart of strawberries, and she will think me greedy. And I do wonder what became of the packet." Then her thoughts went back to the hungry little girl who had disappeared so suddenly, and Ellie realized that she could not ask her grandmother for food to give to the child. "I'll save it. I won't eat so much for my supper and breakfast," she resolved, looking at the deep pocket in her dress and thinking how easy it would be to slip in a piece of bread or cake.

When Ellie went down to supper it was with a troubled heart as to what grandma might say about the strawberries. But she soon realized that Hannah Jane had said nothing about it. And Ellie wished she could let Hannah Jane know how grateful she was; but there was no opportunity. There was hot corn cake for supper, and Ellie liberally buttered a square and slid it into her pocket without grandma's observing it. A slice of gingerbread soon followed, and when Ellie left the supper table her pocket contained enough food to furnish her new friend with a good meal.

But if grandma had not noticed Ellie hiding the food Hannah Jane's eyes had been more alert. As she brought in the tea she had seen Ellie put a piece of cake in her pocket; and when the little girl followed her grandmother from the room Hannah Jane stood looking after them as if too amazed to speak, as indeed she was. Her good impression of Ellie had completely vanished.

"To eat a full quart of strawberries and make a good supper, and then to be sliding food into her pocket," thought Hannah Jane. "Weel, weel! I'll not be surprised to see the doctor in this house before sunrise. But I'll not be worrying the mistress with tales. She'll soon find out by herself," and Hannah Jane went about her duties with a troubled mind.

It was a very uneasy and uncomfortable evening for Ellie. She sat beside her grandmother on the sofa in the big front room, and tried to listen attentively to what Mrs. Hinman was saying. But, looking down to make sure that the contents of her pocket was quite safe, she saw a large spot on the pretty silk. The spot seemed to spread and grow as she looked at it. It was all she could do to sit quietly and not pull out the buttered bread and gingerbread which were spoiling her dress. And she was glad indeed when grandma said it was bedtime.

She went up-stairs very slowly wondering where she should hide the food, and almost ready to cry when she thought of the ugly stain on her new dress.

"I've only been here three days, and all my things are spoiled," she thought bitterly, remembering that one hat was lost, the other crushed out of shape; that her shoes had been ruined by the water, and now here was the pretty flecked silk stained. It seemed to Ellie that there was nothing pleasant to think about. She looked about the shadowy chamber, and decided to put the food in the lower drawer of the tall chest which stood between the two windows. She pulled the drawer open a little way and laid the crushed corn cake and gingerbread in very carefully. In the morning she would get a piece of paper and wrap them up with

what she could save from her breakfast. Ellie was
rather hungry, for she had eaten only a little cold cus-
tard at supper.

Her own troubles and the little brown girl in the
strawberry bed had made her almost forget her father's
namesake and the loss of his packet. But she was too
sleepy to think out any way of helping "Brownie," as
she called the queer little child, and the lost message
seemed beyond help.

CHAPTER X

BRAVE DEEDS

ELLIE was up in good season the next morning, and came down to breakfast looking very neat in her pretty gingham dress with its wide white collar.

"I sat down on my hat, grandma, and it is all bent!" she announced, as she came into the dining-room. But grandma did not seem to think that a very alarming thing. She laughed and said that no doubt she could easily fix it. But Ellie saw Hannah Jane shake her head mournfully, as if all sorts of trouble was to be expected; and she looked at Ellie so sharply that the little girl could feel her cheeks flush.

"Are ye well this morning, Miss Ellen?" she asked, as if surprised to see Ellie down-stairs.

Ellie was more careful this morning. She managed to wrap a couple of pieces of bread in her handkerchief, and when she ran up-stairs to put on her hat she pulled open the drawer and drew out the other things, and then looked about for something to wrap them in. There was a fine piece of tissue paper in her bandbox, and she hurriedly pulled it out and wrapped it about the food just as her grandmother came into the room.

"Now let me see the hat," she said. "I can soon remedy that, my dear," and with a few careful touches the silk hat seemed quite as good as ever.

"I will put on my own bonnet, and then we will start," said Mrs. Hinman, wondering why Ellie stood so close to the wall with both hands behind her.

As soon as Mrs. Hinman left the room Ellie ran down the stairs, through the dining-room into the garden. She was sure that "Brownie" would be lurking somewhere about, and she ran through the flower garden straight toward the strawberry bed, and stood there a moment looking at the high brick wall and wondering how any one could ever get over it. Then suddenly she heard a little chuckle and looked down to see a small brown figure close to the wall.

"Oh, Brownie! Here is all I could get," said Ellie, holding out the package. "And run home just as fast as you can. Don't come in the garden again. I'll come to your house tomorrow."

The child grasped the package eagerly.

"Will you come to-night?" she asked. "I live in Brown Lane. 'Tain't far off. It's the last house."

"Yes, I will come. Truly I will," answered Ellie. "Now run," and Ellie herself turned back toward the house to meet Hannah Jane half-way across the flower garden.

"Ye've not been eating more strawberries, Miss Ellie?" she questioned.

Ellie did not answer. She walked straight on to the hall, where her grandmother was waiting, and in a few moments they were walking across the Square toward Broad Street, and grandma was talking of the shoes they would purchase, and asking Ellie if she would not like a white hat with a wide ribbon of blue silk.

"I think, too, that it will be a good plan for you to have a dress of India muslin," said Mrs. Hinman as they came to the store of Captain Thomas Hopkins, who sold fine India goods.

It seemed very wonderful to Ellie, who had never before been in a shop of any kind, to see shelves filled with cambrics, silks and muslins, and cases of all sorts of things whose names or uses she could not imagine. Mrs. Hinman selected a pretty pale blue India muslin, and then purchased a sash of blue silk to match.

At a milliner's store near by she found just the hat Ellie wanted, and then they visited the shoemaker's, where Ellie was fitted to a pair of low shoes with shining buckles and a pair of fine kid slippers.

With so many things to think about it was no wonder that Ellie forgot all her troubles and was as smiling and happy as ever when she started for home carrying her new shoes and hat, while Mrs. Hinman carried the roll of muslin for the new dress.

"I can make the dress myself, grandma, if you will cut and baste it for me," she said.

"Yes, indeed, dear child. It will be pretty work for you, and with my help 'twill be easily finished," replied Mrs. Hinman.

"Oh! There are Bertha and Mildred," exclaimed Ellie, as they came in sight of the house, and saw the two little Chaplin girls on the porch.

"I asked them to spend the day with you," said Mrs. Hinman. "You may play in the garden, or you may take them up to your room. It will soon be time for dinner."

Ellie was eager to show her friends the purchases her grandmother had made, and both Bertha and Mildred seemed as pleased as Ellie herself. But as Ellie held up the silk sash for their admiration her own smile disappeared.

"Oh, girls!" she exclaimed, "I know a girl who doesn't have any clothes, and who never had enough to eat."

The three little friends were in Ellie's room, and Bertha and Mildred looked at her in surprise as she hurriedly told them the story of the little brown girl whom she had discovered in the strawberry bed.

"Well, Ellie! There's a 'true deed,' I'm sure," declared Mildred as she finished. "You let Hannah Jane blame you and never said a word."

"I promised to go to her house to-night, but if I do you girls will have to help me," said Ellie.

Bertha nodded gravely. "Don't you see that it is our vow to help each other in all brave and true deeds?" she said. "Of course we will help you, and we'll take her some of Nancy's clothes. I think it's fine for you not to eat all you want, Ellie, but to save it for the little girl. We will do that too. But we must keep it a secret."

"Yes, indeed," answered Ellie.

"Of course we can't save any of our dinner to-day, because we are company," said Mildred, and the others agreed to this very promptly.

"What is her name?" asked Bertha.

"I didn't have time to ask her. But she was so brown—hair, eyes, skin and dress—that I called her 'Brownie,' and she lives in Brown Lane," answered Ellie.

"I know where that is," said Bertha. "It leads down to Little River."

Hannah Jane kept a sharp eye on Ellie all through dinner, and was greatly relieved to find that Ellie made no effort to carry off food from the table. Hannah Jane declared to herself that it was more than she could understand why a young lady who was welcome to the best in the house should slip corn-bread into her pocket.

After dinner the girls went out to the arbor and made their plans for the visit to Brown Lane. Bertha said that Lucy and Nancy must be told. "Because they are members of the 'Rose' Society, and because Nancy's dresses will probably fit the little girl," she explained.

"They are coming over this afternoon—your grandma invited them—and we'll tell them all about 'Brownie,'" added Mildred. "Why don't we adopt her?"

Ellie and Bertha both agreed that it would be the right thing to do.

Nancy and Lucy soon arrived, and were greatly excited over Ellie's story of the strange child, and Nancy generously offered to give her any dress that Bertha might decide on.

"But what shall I tell mother?" she asked, a little doubtfully.

"Oh, we must pick out some things of yours that you have outgrown," said Bertha, "and we must do it right away after supper; for Ellie and I are going down to see where this girl lives and carry her something to eat."

"How are you going without any one finding it out?" persisted Nancy.

"Well, after supper I will ask mother if I may run over to see Ellie just a minute, and I know she will let me," answered Bertha, "and I shall wait just beyond the house for Ellie, who will ask her grandma if she may run over to see us, and we will meet and hurry straight off to Brown Lane and get back before any one misses us. Mildred will hide the things we mean to carry near our gate," concluded Bertha.

It all sounded very easy to the girls, and Lucy said that she had two shillings, which were a present from

Grandma Ludlow, that she would give to the adopted child of the "Five Roses." Mildred offered handkerchiefs, and Bertha was sure that she could get a hat from the attic which no one would ever miss. But Ellie had nothing.

"Grandma knows everything I have," she said, "and I haven't any money."

"Never mind. Take her one of Hannah Jane's fine cakes," suggested Mildred. "You can ask Hannah Jane for it as if you wanted to share it with us."

"She will think me very greedy," said Ellie, "for she thinks that I ate a quart of ripe strawberries before supper last night."

"Never mind that," said Bertha. "Of course it will take courage to ask her, but 'twill be another brave deed," so Ellie agreed to ask; but she was sure it would take all her courage.

"We had better go home now and get all the things we can and hide them before supper time," said Mildred; so the sisters bade Ellie good-bye, and Bertha promised to wait for her after supper beyond the Chaplin house gate.

Ellie walked very slowly back to the house. She knew that she must go to the kitchen and ask Hannah Jane for the cake. She said to herself that it was Hannah Jane who had first told her to think about poor children, but she dreaded the scornful look which she had seen in Hannah Jane's eyes only yesterday when they had met in the garden.

The kitchen was in an ell beyond the main house and there was a little porch over the door covered with honeysuckle vines. A neat little brick laid path led to the kitchen door, and Ellie followed it wondering just what she should say.

As she reached the porch she heard Hannah Jane singing:

> "Hark ye all to Freedom's call
> And bravely, bravely sing —"

But Ellie's step on the porch brought Hannah Jane to the door.

"You were singing, weren't you?" said Ellie, trying to smile as if she and Hannah Jane were the best of friends.

"Maybe so, miss; but not neglecting my rightful duties. I can sing and work at the same time," replied Hannah Jane. "Were you wishing anything, Miss Ellen Elizabeth?"

It seemed to Ellie that it was indeed brave to venture to ask a favor from Hannah Jane. Her mouth felt very dry, and she swallowed and hesitated, and at last said:

"Yes; if you please, Hannah Jane, would you kindly give me a whole cake? I told Bertha—"

She stopped suddenly and looked up, for Hannah Jane had made such a queer noise.

"So 'tis a cake ye're wantin'? Weel, heaven grant your grandmither little knows of the cormorant in her house," replied Hannah Jane. "I'll give ye the cake; but mind ye share it with your friends," and Hannah Jane looked sternly down at the frightened little girl.

"Oh, yes, indeed I will, Hannah Jane. I won't eat a speck of it myself," Ellie declared so earnestly that Hannah Jane groaned again, for she was quite sure that Ellie would eat the greater part of the cake herself.

"I'll put a paper over it," she said, and disappeared into the pantry returning in a moment with a neat package which she handed to the little girl.

"Don't be askin' of me again, Miss Ellen Elizabeth," she said sternly, and Ellie thanked her meekly and hurried down the brick walk and around the corner of the house to the open door of the dining-room. She carried the cake to her room, and then went in search of her grandmother, who was in the pleasant sitting-room.

"You must begin your letter to your mother to-morrow," said Mrs. Hinman. "You will have a great deal to tell her."

"Yes, indeed," said Ellie, wishing it were possible to write to her mother about the packet David Barlow had given her.

"There is great news to-day, my dear child," continued Mrs. Hinman. "Two Tory spies have been captured and brought to Hartford. And they say that one of them is only a boy."

"Did Stevie bring him?" Ellie asked, in so eager a voice that her grandmother looked up in surprise.

"Why, no, dear child. The spies were captured in a boat in which they were making their way along the shore. I suppose Stephen wants to help America's cause by securing an enemy spy, does he not?" she answered, and Ellie nodded, half frightened to think how nearly she had disobeyed her father's instructions not to speak of the deserter to any one.

"May I go over to see Bertha for a little while after supper?" she asked, feeling her face flush uncomfortably because she was not being quite truthful to her kind grandmother who had given her so many pretty things that very day.

Mrs. Hinman gave her consent, and Ellie started off as soon after supper as she could escape Hannah Jane's watchful eyes, carrying the cake very carefully.

CHAPTER XI

THE MYSTERIOUS PACKAGE

BERTHA was waiting, standing in the shadow of one of the big elm trees. In one hand she carried a wide-rimmed hat trimmed with white ribbon, while a good-sized basket rested on the ground beside her.

"I have a lot of things," she whispered, as soon as Ellie came near. "Put your cake in the basket and help me carry it." Ellie promptly obeyed, and the two little girls hurried down the shadowy street, and in a short time had reached Brown Lane, which proved to be only a rough path toward Little River. They had just turned into the lane when a little figure came running to meet them.

"I was just watching for you," she declared, hopping about first on one foot and then on the other.

"This is my house," she continued, pointing to a low shed-like building. "An' Joe's waitin'. I told him you'd come, but he didn't believe it."

"We must hurry back just as fast as we can," said Bertha. "Here is a hat for you, and there are a dress and some shoes in the basket."

"And a cake," Ellie added eagerly.

"Oh, yes; there's part of a chicken, too, and some cookies," said Bertha, "and here are two shillings my sister sent you."

By this time they had reached the door of the child's home, and Bertha set down the basket, handed her first the hat and then the money.

"What is your name?" Bertha asked.

"It's May," replied the child, in a husky voice. "What's yours?"

"Rose. That is, you may call us both Rose," replied Bertha. "We must not stay a minute. We'll come again," and taking Ellie's hand she turned back. But in an instant "Brownie" was beside Ellie, whispering in her ear:

"Thank you, thank you, thank you. Come to-morrow," and before Ellie could answer she was gone.

"I do hope they haven't missed us," Bertha said anxiously, as the two little girls hurried along the rough lane. "I have been thinking about Fort Danger; that will be a good place to meet May, and to leave things for her. We must tell her about it to-morrow."

They ran nearly all the way home, and it was a very flushed and tired little girl who went slowly up the steps to Mrs. Hinman's porch.

"I was just about going over to come home with you," said Grandma Hinman. "Why, dear child, you should not have run home. You were not frightened, I trust."

"Oh, no," Ellie panted, "I—I just wanted to run."

"Well, to-morrow we will begin on the new dress. But what do you think? Hannah Jane tells me that some one has picked the very best of my strawberries!"

Ellie did not speak. She wondered why Hannah Jane had not told her grandmother of finding her in the strawberry bed. She wished that she could tell grandma all the story; but she must not do that unless little brown "May" and the "Roses" would give their consent. Ellie began to feel as if too many things were happening.

The next morning Ellie began a letter to her mother, telling her of her safe and pleasant journey in the coach, of making the acquaintance of Mrs. Ludlow, and of her new playmates, the little Chaplin girls. She sent messages to her father and brothers. Then she thought of Barlay. Suppose, after all, that the errand he had trusted her to do was a harmless one? Perhaps the little package might have contained money to purchase something that he might need, and which he would expect to receive by the coach which carried her letter.

Ellie was sitting at her grandmother's desk in the front room, and with Grandmother Hinman's new quill pen in her hand; but all her pleasure in her neatly written letter to her dear mother was at an end.

"I must find it," she declared, jumping up from the desk and running up-stairs to her room. Hannah Jane was just coming out from the chamber.

"I have been sweeping your room. Have ye missed a small package, Miss Ellen Elizabeth?" she asked, looking so sternly at the little girl that Ellie wondered how any one could really like Hannah Jane; but at the question Ellie's face brightened.

"Oh, yes, Hannah Jane, and I looked everywhere for it," she answered.

"Did ye? Weel, 'twas lying on the closet floor beside your bandbox. An' I have placed it on the light-stand," replied Hannah Jane.

Ellie ran past her into the room, and there lay the lost package on the stand. She took it up and looked at it carefully. There were a few words written on the wrapper, and Ellie read these aloud:

"'Miss Ellen Elizabeth Barlow. Please open as soon as you reach Hartford.'

"Oh!" exclaimed the little girl, now quite sure that Barlay's errand was an innocent one, "and I have been here nearly a week," she thought. But whatever the message might be she did not want to open the package before Hannah Jane, who had now returned to the room.

"I'll be dusting as soon as ye're pleased to step down-stairs, Miss Ellen Elizabeth," said Hannah Jane.

Ellie moved quickly toward the door, thrusting the newly-found package into her pocket. Whenever Hannah Jane said "Miss Ellen Elizabeth" Ellie felt as if it were a reproach to her for some unacknowledged fault.

Ellie ran down-stairs and out to the arbor. She looked carefully about, but there was no one to be seen, so she sat down on the bench and untied the string which held the package. After taking off the stout paper in which it was wrapped Ellie found there were two other packages. One was a neatly folded letter, the other a thick little package, and on this was written her name, and: "Please buy something you want with this." Ellie opened it quickly, and there lay a golden sovereign. She looked at it in amazement. It seemed untold riches to the little girl, who had never before had more than a silver sixpence of her very own. She was sure that it would purchase everything that a little girl could possibly want. Holding it tight in one hand she now looked down at the address on the letter, and read aloud: "To His Excellency Governor Jonathan Trumbull." Then further down was written: "Important. Deliver as soon as possible."

Ellie put the letter and its wrappings and her gold piece into her pocket. "'As soon as possible,'" she repeated. Why, that meant now. At once. No spy would send a letter to the loyal governor of Connecticut. Young as she was Ellie understood that at once. And it was marked "Important." Ellie began to feel that it was really a wonderful thing to be trusted to deliver a message to Governor Jonathan Trumbull. As she sat thinking how she could fulfil this trust Peter passed the arbor on his way to the vegetable garden.

"Peter," called Ellie, running after him, "will you please tell me where Governor Trumbull lives?"

"To be sure, Miss Ellen. He lives in the fine town of Lebanon. That's where he has his store, and his War Office; and 'tis from there he sends out the wagon-trains of provisions for American soldiers," replied Peter, evidently greatly pleased to be able to answer Ellie's question.

"Oh! Then I can't see him," responded Ellie in so mournful a tone that Peter realized the little girl was greatly disappointed, and he smiled and nodded reassuringly.

"To be sure you can see him," he declared. "He is in Hartford this very week to attend the General Assembly."

"I wish I could see him," Ellie exclaimed earnestly.

That Ellie should wish to see Governor Trumbull seemed a very right and proper thing to Peter. Did not

General Washington declare that Connecticut's governor was "among the first of patriots"? He looked at Ellie approvingly.

"If you should ask your Grandmother Hinman I've no doubt she would take you down to see Governor Trumbull enter Assembly Hall. He will be going in at one o'clock this day," said Peter, nodding pleasantly, as he started on to his work.

"'At one o'clock this day,'" Ellie repeated. Dinner would be over long before that, and she resolved to slip away by herself and find out by asking some one on the street the way to Assembly Hall; then she would watch for the governor and give him Barlay's message. "Probably it's to say that he is sorry he fought against Connecticut, and to ask the governor if he may stay with my father," thought the little girl hopefully. The discovery of the mysterious packet, and finding out that it held no harmful message, made Ellie very happy indeed. She was sure that it would be very easy to hand a letter to Governor Trumbull; and the golden sovereign, she had already decided, should be used to buy a fine present for her mother. She turned back to the house feeling that now she would enjoy every minute of her visit, and for the time quite forgetting the little brown girl whom she had promised to visit.

Hannah Jane stood just inside the dining-room door.

"Your grandmother wishes you to step up-stairs to her chamber, Miss Ellen Elizabeth," she said grimly.

"Yes, Hannah Jane," Ellie responded smilingly, so that Hannah Jane's face softened a little as she turned to look after her.

The blue India muslin was spread out on Mrs. Hinman's bed.

"I am going to cut off the breadths for your skirt, my dear," said grandma. "Why, you look as if you had heard some good news," she added smilingly.

While Mrs. Hinman cut off the lengths of soft muslin Ellie looked about the big chamber. There was a portrait of Grandfather Hinman hanging over the mantel, and in the corner of the room was a wooden cradle. Ellie looked at it wonderingly.

"Your dear mother slept in that cradle when she was a baby," said grandma, who had noticed Ellie's questioning look. "And now, my dear, I will baste up the seams, and after dinner you can begin work on your new dress."

"I wish I could see Governor Trumbull," Ellie said, in so sober a tone that her grandmother looked up quickly.

"Of course it would be something to tell your brothers of when you go home," grandma replied, "and I doubt not the governor would be glad to see you, my child, for your grandfather was his good friend when they were both young. And there is the bell for our dinner," she concluded, as the silvery tinkle sounded from the lower hall, and Ellie followed her grandmother down to the dining-room. She was very quiet during the meal, and as soon as it was over slipped away up-stairs.

"I shall have to leave you alone with your work for an hour, my dear," said Mrs. Hinman, as they left the dining-room. "I want to assist Hannah Jane in the kitchen."

It seemed to Ellie that nothing could be more fortunate for her plan. She ran up-stairs, put on the new hat with its ribbon of blue silk, and in a few moments she had reached the square and was hurrying toward Broad Street, feeling sure that she would meet some one who would direct her to Assembly Hall.

CHAPTER XII

ELLIE AND GOVERNOR TRUMBULL

ELLIE had just turned on to Broad Street when she saw a little girl coming toward her. The little girl wore a white straw hat trimmed with white ribbon, and a dress of figured muslin. There was something familiar to Ellie about this little girl, but not until they were face to face did she realize that it was May.

"Oh! Were you coming to see me?" exclaimed May. "See! Isn't my hat fine? And my dress?" she continued, without waiting for Ellie to answer her first question. "I never had a hat before in all my life," she concluded, touching the brim of the white straw as if it was something very precious.

"No, I wasn't going to see you, May. I am going to see Governor Trumbull," replied Ellie.

"You will have to hurry, then, for I have just seen him on his way to Assembly Hall. Come, I'll show you," replied May, taking hold of Ellie's hand, and turning back. "We shall have to run," she said, and without another word the two little girls ran down the street. May evidently was familiar with every turn of the streets. They passed several little groups of people, and in a few moments they came to a full stop. "Look! There he comes. See those soldiers?" and she pointed to several men, headed by two American soldiers, who were just then crossing the street very near to where they were standing.

"Which one is Governor Trumbull?" asked Ellie.

"The slender man with the three-cornered hat and the long coat. The one who looks so sober," replied May.

It seemed to Ellie that all the men in the little group led by the soldiers looked sober; but May's pointing finger left no doubt as to which one was Governor Jonathan Trumbull, and greatly to May's amazement Ellie darted forward, and in a moment was standing beside the governor, looking up into the grave kindly face, whose dark eyes and firm mouth softened as Ellie held out the letter and said, in a voice so low that it could hardly be heard:

"If you please, sir, this is a message for you."

The moment the letter was in the governor's hand Ellie turned and fled down the street. May was close behind her, but neither of them spoke. May was so nearly overcome with half-terrified admiration of Ellie's courage in daring to approach the governor of Connecticut that she could not speak; and all Ellie could think of was that she must get home as quickly as pos-

"THIS IS A MESSAGE FOR YOU"

sible. It did not occur to her that Governor Trumbull might wish to question her, or to send some answer to the letter which she had given him.

"You're going straight away from home," May said at last, just as Ellie realized that she could not run another step.

"Oh, dear! Why didn't you tell me before?" responded Ellie. "Where are we?" and she looked around curiously, realizing that she had never been in that part of the town before.

"We're nearly at the ferry. See, there is the river. I know a way across the fields that will bring us to the back of your garden," said May, looking at her new friend with admiring eyes.

"I'm so tired. I wish I could rest a minute," said Ellie, looking about as if in search of some place where she could sit down.

"Let's crawl under this fence, then we can sit down on the grass," suggested May, pointing to a high rail fence which separated the road from a field, and at the same time moving toward it. Ellie followed slowly, and the two girls had no trouble in crawling under the lower rail. They were both very warm, and were glad of the shade of a wide-spreading maple tree which grew near by.

"Did you write the letter to Governor Trumbull?" asked May as they sat down.

Ellie shook her head. "No, it's a secret. I guess it's something I can't tell even the Roses," she responded. "What is your name besides 'May'?"

"My name is May Vincent. But you called me 'Brownie' at first. I wish you would always call me that," replied May.

Ellie agreed to do this, and told Brownie her own name, and that she was on a visit to her grandmother. As the two girls sat resting in the shade they learned a great deal about each other. May said that she was ten years old, and that her brother Joe was eight. And Ellie told her new friend about her own brothers, her mother and father, and her pleasant home in the country.

"What did the girl who came with you yesterday mean when she told me to call you both 'Rose'?" questioned Brownie.

"Oh, that's our secret name for each other, and for Bertha's sisters," Ellie explained; and then, realizing suddenly how long a time she had been away from home, she jumped up and said: "We must hurry. I ought not to have rested so long."

"It isn't so very far across the fields," declared Brownie, leading the way.

"I am so glad I met you, Brownie; I don't believe I should have been in time to meet Governor Trumbull if you had not told me to hurry and then pointed him out to me," said Ellie.

For a moment Brownie did not reply. She was wishing with all her heart that she had gone hungry rather than to have taken the strawberries from her friend's garden. Then she remembered that Ellie had helped her pick them for Joe, and the thought comforted her.

As they walked along together near the bank of the river Ellie began to look about, thinking that, after all, she knew the place.

"I have been here before. Look, Brownie," and she pointed up to a steep bank not far distant. "There is Fort Danger. That is where the Chaplin girls go to talk secrets; and Bertha said it would be just the place for you to come and meet us. Come on, I'll show you how to get there," and quite forgetting that she was in a hurry to reach home Ellie started off toward Fort Danger.

"We can't climb up there," said Brownie.

"No, but we can go through the field and slide down," replied Ellie.

It did not take them long to reach the top of the slope, and Ellie explained just how to slide down to Fort Danger.

"Hush," whispered Brownie, who had been peering over the top, "there's some one down there now."

Ellie lay down beside Brownie and looked over. Then she laughed delightedly. "It's the 'Roses,'" she whispered. "We'll slide down and surprise them. You go first."

Almost before she had finished speaking Brownie had gone sliding down the steep bank, quickly followed by Ellie.

There was a chorus of surprised shouts from the Chaplin girls, and then Bertha exclaimed: "Why, it's May and Ellie, and I was just telling Nancy and Lucy about you," and she nodded smilingly toward Brownie.

"Are you just as old as I?" asked Nancy, noticing that her dress fitted the stranger as if it had been made for her.

"I'm past ten," replied Brownie.

"We came here to-day on purpose to plan about you, May," said Bertha. "We don't mean to let you be hungry again. And we have taken a vow that you shall have clothes. We called for you, Ellie," she continued, turning toward her friend, "but Hannah Jane said that you were to sew for an hour."

"Oh!" gasped Ellie, who had entirely forgotten the blue India muslin, "what will my grandma think! I never set a stitch. What time is it?"

"It must be four o'clock," Bertha answered, looking at Ellie and wondering where she could have been all the afternoon.

"I must not stay another minute," declared Ellie, starting for the edge of the terrace.

Bertha and Mildred both decided that it was time for them all to go home. Before they left the fort Bertha showed "Brownie," as the "Roses" had decided to call their new friend, a small flat rock close against the steep bank. On lifting the rock a good sized cavity appeared.

"Some of us will come every day and leave something there for you, Brownie," Bertha promised, "and if you get into any trouble or want us for anything, you can leave a note there for us."

"I can't write!" Brownie declared in so tragic a tone that the little girls all looked at each other as if questioning what was to be done.

"I can't either," declared Lucy, "but Bertha is teaching me."

"We'll teach you, Brownie," Mildred and Ellie both exclaimed, and then with promises to meet at the fort early in the afternoon of the next day, the little girls slid down the bank to the river path and started for home.

To Brownie it had been the happiest day that she could remember. She had been neatly dressed, she had helped Ellie to deliver a message to the governor, and, best of all, she thought, she had been welcomed as a friend and playmate by girls of her own age; none of whom had made fun of her poverty or run away from her, as had happened to her in times past. For May Vincent had known but little of the kindness and happiness that most children enjoy. Her mother had died when she was a very small child, and her father with his two children had moved from place to place, never staying in one town long enough to make friends who would interest themselves in his children. And now here were five girls who had promised that she should have food and clothes, and who seemed to like her. Brownie fairly danced along the river path toward her home. She had already told Joe and her father that two girls had given her the food and clothes. She wished that she could tell them about the fort, but she realized that Fort Danger was a secret which she had been trusted not to betray.

She was crossing the field where she and Ellie had rested, and stopped for a moment in the shade of the big maple. Then she crawled under the fence, and saw something golden and bright almost under her hand.

"It's a piece of gold money!" she exclaimed, picking it up and looking at it with shining happy eyes. "It must be a lot of money. Enough to buy some clothes for Joe. I've found it, so it's mine."

Holding it tight in her hand she ran swiftly toward home, thinking of all the wonderful things that were coming into her life. As she neared the tumble-down shack she could see her father sitting in the doorway with Joe beside him.

"Perhaps father will stay here now. I do hope he will," she thought, waving her hand toward Joe, who was running to meet her.

But Ellie did not approach home with any such delight. She walked soberly along beside Bertha, wondering what her Grandmother Hinman must think of a little girl who ran away without a word of excuse or explanation. And Hannah Jane! How could she dare to face Hannah Jane!

CHAPTER XIII

THE SPARE ROOM

GRANDMA HINMAN had not been greatly troubled when she discovered that Ellie was not in her room sewing on the blue muslin. She knew that the Chaplin girls had called for Ellie, and, not hearing Hannah Jane's reply to their inquiry, had taken it for granted that her little granddaughter had gone out to play with her friends.

"'Tis a warm day for the child to sit indoors, and I am glad she is out with her young friends," thought the good-natured old lady. Mrs. Ludlow came over with her knitting and the time had passed quickly, so when Ellie came running into the cool sitting-room, half afraid of what her grandmother might say to her, she found two smiling old ladies who welcomed her with friendly questions about her afternoon's pleasure.

"Sit here by me, dear child," said Mrs. Ludlow; "we have hardly seen each other since our stage-coach journey. But I have not forgotten my promise to take you on a visit to the Charter Oak."

Ellie's hands and face were dirty, her shoes were dusty, and there were grass stains on the white dress.

118

Her new hat was perched over one ear, and her hair was ruffled. She was so tired that she wondered how she could ever walk across the room to the big sofa where Mrs. Ludlow was sitting. And at that moment she suddenly remembered the golden sovereign, and thrust her hand into her pocket to make sure of its safety. It was the first time she had thought of it since handing Governor Trumbull the letter from Barlay. In an instant Ellie realized that it was lost. Her pocket was empty; and quite forgetting her grandmother and Mrs. Ludlow she exclaimed: "Oh! I've lost it! I've lost it!"

When Mrs. Hinman had noticed Ellie's untidy condition, her smile had faded; and when Ellie failed to curtsy to Mrs. Ludlow her face had grown stern. Now at Ellie's outcry she said:

"Ellen, run up-stairs at once and stay until I call you."

For a moment Ellie stood as if she had not quite understood her grandmother's words. In all her life she had never before been sent from a room. She felt ashamed and ill-treated, and left the room quickly. She could hardly see the stairs through her tears as she made her way to her room. She pushed open the door and entered. The room was very dark. The windows were closed and the curtains closely drawn. But the little girl hardly noticed this. She made her way to the big bed and flung herself across it, sobbing bitterly.

"It's all because of that old message. I wish Barlay had never come to our house," she thought. The golden sovereign with which she had meant to buy a present for her mother was lost, her grandmother had sent her from the room, and she was sure that Hannah Jane did not like her; all these things taken together seemed more trouble than Ellie could bear. She resolved to ask her grandmother if she could not go home. A coach would leave for Salisbury the next day. "I know my mother will be glad to see me," was Ellie's last waking thought, for she was so tired, and the big bed was so comfortable that she was off to sleep in a very short time.

"We will not call Ellen to supper. I was obliged to send her to her room," said Grandma Hinman when Hannah Jane said that supper was ready.

Hannah Jane nodded approvingly. It seemed to her that it was a good opportunity to tell Mrs. Hinman that it was Ellen who had taken the strawberries. "So she'll na be doubtin' the honesty of other folk," thought Hannah Jane; so she told of finding Ellie in the strawberry bed, and added that she had seen Ellie slip bread and cake into her pocket at the table, and that Ellie had asked for a whole cake which she had taken to her own room. "I had na doubt the lassie would be sick," Hannah Jane concluded.

Mrs. Hinman listened as if she could hardly believe her own ears. She loved her little granddaughter dearly, and it was hard to think that Ellie could have done all the things of which Hannah Jane accused her; but Mrs. Hinman knew that Hannah Jane was absolutely to be trusted, and she could see that the old Scotchwoman felt very bad to have such a tale to tell.

"I cannot understand it. She seemed such a dear child," said grandmother, who was nearly ready to cry when she thought that her own daughter's little girl could be so unworthy of her confidence.

"I will go up-stairs a little later, and have a talk with the child. Perhaps there is some explanation for her conduct," she said, but she had little appetite for the excellent supper which Hannah Jane had prepared.

It was twilight when Grandma Hinman, carrying a little silver tray on which was a bowl of bread and milk and a plate of freshly made gingerbread, entered Ellie's room. The windows toward the garden were open, and the fragrance of many flowers came into the shadowy room. Grandma set the tray on a table and then tiptoed toward the bed, thinking that Ellie might be asleep.

The bed was smooth and undisturbed. The big pillows had not been touched. Grandma looked anxiously around the room; there was no trace of Ellie. Frightened and anxious, she hurried to the kitchen.

"Hannah Jane, Ellie is not in her room. I am afraid she did not go up-stairs at all."

Mrs. Hinman's voice trembled, and her face was very white. Perhaps Ellie had been ill after all, out of her head and feverish, and had not known what she was doing, and had now wandered off, thought grandma.

"She's not gone far. Like as not she's stepped out to the garden where it is cool," replied Hannah Jane, apparently not at all disturbed by Ellie's disappearance. But when a thorough search of the garden failed to discover the missing girl, and when Peter returned from the Chaplins' saying that Ellie was not there, even Hannah Jane became alarmed. It did not occur to any of them that the little girl could be sound asleep in the big spare room, which was never opened unless distinguished visitors arrived, but into which Ellie had stumbled, not knowing where she went, and thinking only of her troubles.

The Chaplins all joined in the search. A constable was called, and went through the streets ringing a bell and calling: "Lost child! Lost child! A little girl ten years old. Lost child!" But the summer night went by and morning came, and Grandma Hinman, sad and nearly ill with anxiety, sat in the big front room waiting for some news of Ellie.

It was sunrise before Hannah Jane could persuade her to go to bed, and even then she would not go to her own room. "Open the windows in the spare room, Hannah Jane. Perhaps I'll sleep if I do not go to my own bed," she said mournfully, reproaching herself for her sternness toward Ellie.

Hannah Jane found the door of the room ajar and went in quietly. She did not feel quite happy when she remembered her own behavior toward Ellie. "I might have been a bit kinder, maybe," she said to herself, as she drew back the chintz curtains, and opened the windows. Then she turned toward the bed.

"Powers defend us!" she whispered, as she saw Ellie, who had not taken off the dusty shoes or the soiled dress, lying across the bed.

"An' me, the loony, never to look in this room," muttered Hannah Jane as she hastened down-stairs.

"'Tis me fault, ma'am. Miss Ellen Elizabeth is in the spare room fast asleep with her shoes on, and me never thinking to look there for her," she declared. Before Hannah Jane had finished speaking Mrs. Hinman was hurrying up the stairs into the big chamber, and stood looking down at the tear-stained little face.

"Can you take off her shoes without waking her?" she whispered to Hannah Jane, who nodded with a little smile on her grim face. Then, very carefully, the two women undressed the little girl, slipped on her night-dress, and Ellie, with a little murmuring sigh of comfort, rested between the lavender-scented sheets.

"I'll lie down beside the child," said Mrs. Hinman, and Hannah Jane nodded understandingly, and closed the door softly behind her.

When Ellie awoke some hours later she looked about her in astonishment. She had never seen this room before. "Oh!" she exclaimed, when she found that Grandma Hinman was lying beside her fast asleep. "I guess I haven't waked up after all. Perhaps Brownie is a dream, too. Perhaps I didn't find her picking grandma's nice strawberries, and perhaps I didn't ask Hannah Jane for a cake to give her; and perhaps—" but Grandma Hinman had opened her eyes and was smiling at her. Mrs. Hinman had heard every word.

"Tell me all about Brownie, dear child," she said gently. "I am glad you gave her a cake. Tell me about her, and we will ask her to come and make us a visit. She is welcome to the berries."

"Oh, grandma! Truly?" and with her head resting beside Grandma Hinman's Ellie told Brownie's story, and of the things that the Chaplin girls had given her. "And we have adopted her," she concluded. And grandma said that the story had made her very happy, and promised to ask Brownie to come for a lesson in writing each day.

"And grandma, there's another secret that I can't tell. It's about Governor Trumbull," concluded Ellie.

But grandma laughed, and said that any secret about the governor must surely not be told, so that the little girl felt that all her troubles were over. She was sorry about the lost gold piece, but now that grandma knew all about Brownie the lost money seemed of small importance.

"I must tell Hannah Jane," grandma said. "I cannot have her blame you unjustly," and Ellie agreed. She wondered why she had not told her grandmother at once. Ellie knew that the "Five Roses" would understand. She had not betrayed any of their secrets; and as Brownie was her discovery Ellie decided that she had the right to tell Grandma Hinman about her.

"Weel, now, Miss Ellie!" was Hannah Jane's smiling greeting when the little girl followed her grandmother into the dining-room that morning.

"You know, Hannah Jane, you said it would 'become' me to think of little girls who had not shoes or a hat to their feet," Ellie reminded her, and Hannah Jane nodded.

"I'd 'a' made a bigger cake, had ye but told me," she replied.

CHAPTER XIV

A VISITOR

GOVERNOR TRUMBULL opened and read the letter which Ellie had thrust into his hand before he reached Assembly Hall, and his companions noticed that he was even more grave than usual. For the letter warned him that a party of Tories were planning to seize him and deliver him as a prisoner to the British.

Governor Jonathan Trumbull had been a special object of the enemy's vengeance because of his unfaltering patriotism. But this was the first warning that he had received of his own personal danger.

"Who was the child who handed me this note?" he asked, turning to one of his companions.

"There were two little girls, Your Excellency," responded the man, who was a resident of Hartford. "I think one of them lives in Brown Lane, but the other child I have never seen."

"They must be found at once," declared the governor. "Lose no time in sending men in search of them. And bring them to my lodging. Read this," and he handed the letter to his companion. So that while Ellie and Brownie were at Fort Danger the streets of

Hartford were being searched for them, and Mr. Vincent had been sharply questioned as to the whereabouts of his small daughter, and as to his knowledge of her companions.

It was at a time when British ships were cruising up and down the Connecticut coast, sweeping it clear of American vessels, and plundering the seaport towns. Often these craft made their way into the Connecticut River, and the inhabitants of all the river towns were constantly on the alert for the enemy. Many British prisoners of war were held in Hartford, and it was sometimes feared that these men had some way of communicating with their friends, and giving information as to American supplies of powder which were stored in that town. And Governor Trumbull thought it possible that this mysterious message must have been written by some one who was familiar with the enemy's plans. His personal guard was at once increased, and precautions taken to protect the buildings where the powder was stored. Meanwhile the governor waited for some news of the children who had brought the letter, and late in the afternoon May Vincent, accompanied by her father and brother, was brought to him, and the gentleman who had walked beside the governor declared that May was one of the girls who had approached Governor Trumbull on his way to the General Assembly, and had handed him the letter.

Poor Brownie was thoroughly frightened, but determined that whatever happened to her she would not betray Ellie. She was almost glad of the opportunity of showing her loyalty to her friend. And she would not answer any question in regard to her companion of the afternoon. Her father and little Joe waited for her at the entrance to the governor's house, both greatly alarmed but sure that it must be a mistake.

Governor Trumbull had questioned her himself, and at last said:

"My child, you need not be afraid that I mean any harm to the little girl who gave me the letter. It is quite the contrary. She did me a great favor. I want to see her and thank her, and, if possible, reward her. It is possible that she has saved my life."

At these words May looked up at the grave friendly face, whose dark eyes rested upon her so kindly. She did not question his words or their meaning. She was sure that he could be trusted, and she now was eager to tell all she knew about Ellie. Beginning with their meeting in Mrs. Hinman's strawberry bed she told of Ellie's kindness to her, and of her wish to give the letter into his own hands.

The governor had smiled at the mention of the name of Mrs. Hinman, but he was still curious as to who had written the letter.

"Madame Hinman is an old and valued friend, and I am glad that the letter comes from one of her family," he said as May finished.

"Now, my child, you have conferred a favor on me, and I wish to reward you. What shall I give you for yourself?"

May smiled with delight.

"If you please, sir, would you shake hands with my father? He is waiting for me, and it would make him proud indeed," she said.

"You are a good child," responded Governor Trumbull, leading the way to the door, where Mr. Vincent stood waiting. The governor noticed that the man was lame and poorly clothed, and that the little boy was ragged.

"Your little daughter has asked me to shake hands with you, Mr. Vincent," he said smilingly, and their hands met in a firm clasp. Then with a friendly word to Joe and May, His Excellency bade them good-night, and returned to his sitting-room.

"I will call on Madame Hinman to-morrow, and make the acquaintance of her granddaughter," he thought, as he sat down at his desk, "and I must see if I cannot find employment for this Vincent. He has not been fortunate."

May's father heard the story of Ellie and the letter as the little family walked back to the tumble-down house in Brown Lane.

"'Tis a proud day for me," the lame man declared. "I never expected to shake hands with Jonathan Trumbull. See that you always remember this day, children." And then May showed them the golden sovereign which she had found, and her father agreed that on the next day they would buy clothes for little Joe.

"Maybe better times are coming to us. If I could but get steady work we'd do nicely," said Mr. Vincent.

At an early hour the next morning, Governor Trumbull, accompanied by an armed escort, arrived at the brick mansion-house on Market Square, and when Hannah Jane opened the front door and confronted the governor she was nearly speechless with surprise.

"Will you ask your mistress if she will see Jonathan Trumbull?" said the governor.

"Yes, Your Excellency," stammered Hannah Jane, with a stiff curtsy. "Will you please to step in?"

Governor Trumbull entered the cool parlor, while Hannah Jane hastened away to find Mrs. Hinman and tell her the wonderful news. Years ago, Hannah Jane remembered, the governor and his young daughter had been there, but then he was only "young Mr. Trumbull," the son of a prosperous merchant; but now all Connecticut trusted in his judgment and energy to preserve their freedom.

It seemed to Hannah Jane that her mistress received the news that the governor of Connecticut was waiting in her parlor in much too calm a manner. "Quite as if governors and princes were always making morning calls in this house," thought the elderly Scotchwoman. But Miss Ellen Elizabeth was apparently frightened.

"Oh, grandmother! Has he come to see me?" she asked, looking as if she were ready to cry.

Mrs. Hinman smiled at the little girl's excitement. "Why, my dear, you need not be frightened. Only yesterday you were wishing that you might see Governor Trumbull, and here he is in our parlor this very minute," and taking Ellie by the hand she led her down the stairs and into the big front room.

Mrs. Hinman was greatly pleased and honored that her old friend had taken time to call upon her. But she was greatly surprised when, taking Ellie's hand, he smiled down upon the little girl and said:

"It is really Miss Ellen Elizabeth Barlow whom I came to see," and then he handed Mrs. Hinman the letter, and told her that Ellie had given it to him yesterday on his way to the General Assembly.

"Why, where did you get this, Ellie?" Grandma Hinman questioned. "I knew nothing of this, Mr. Trumbull," she said.

"Oh, grandma, it's a secret," Ellie pleaded. "My mother and father both told me not to tell."

"Did your father send me the letter?" questioned the governor. "It was a friendly act, from whomever it came," he added quickly, "but I must try my best to discover who wrote it, for I feel sure he can give me valuable information. Perhaps if your father and mother knew that it was the governor of Connecticut who asked your confidence they would bid you to tell me all you can."

"I am sure they would," said Grandma Hinman. "Tell our friend just who gave you the letter, dear child, and all you know about it. I will make it right with your father and mother."

So Ellie, sitting on the big sofa beside Governor Trumbull, with her hand resting in his, told him the story of Stephen's prisoner. That his name was the same as that of her father, and that the boys called him "Barlay."

"He knows about stars, and silkworms, and birds and plants," she added, and then told of her putting his package in her bandbox, and how frightened she had been when she thought it was lost.

"There was a golden sovereign for me in the package, but I put it in my pocket and lost it," said Ellie as she finished the story.

"And so this was your secret about Governor Trumbull?" said grandma smilingly. "Well, my dear, I think you have proved that you can be trusted with secrets."

The governor said that later on he must see the young deserter from the British Army and question him. "I can trust David Barlow and his family to keep him safely until that time," he added.

Ellie listened while Governor Trumbull told Mrs. Hinman of an ingenious contrivance for damaging ships of the enemy which had just been brought to his notice by a Mr. Bushnell from Saybrook.

"It is a machine not unlike a large turtle. In the head is an opening, sufficiently large to admit a man. This apartment is air-tight, but is supplied with sufficient air to support life for thirty minutes. The operator has oar and rudder to direct his course. At the bottom is an aperture, with a valve, to admit water, so that the 'turtle' can submerge, and two pumps to eject the water, when necessary to rise to the surface.

"Behind the 'head,'" continued Governor Trumbull, who was evidently greatly interested in the "turtle," "and above the rudder, is a place for carrying a large powder magazine. This is made of two pieces of oak timber, hollowed out, and large enough to hold one hundred and fifty pounds of powder, with the apparatus for firing it, and can be located in any place where it is designed to act by means of a screw turned by the operator. Within the powder magazine is a piece of clockwork, capable of running twelve hours. The operator can set this, a sort of gun-lock, and be safely away before the explosion takes place," concluded Governor Trumbull, rising to his feet and declaring that he must hasten away.

"These 'turtles' may do good service in protecting our coast and harbors," he added, and smiled down at Ellie, who thought this must be the most wonderful machine that was ever made. He thanked her very gravely for the service she had rendered him, and Ellie and Mrs. Hinman walked with him to the porch, where they both made their best curtsy, and then stood watching him as, with his guard, he walked down the street.

"My dear, we have been greatly honored this morning," said Grandma Hinman, as she and Ellie returned to the parlor, "and I am proud indeed that my little granddaughter could be of service to so true a patriot as Jonathan Trumbull."

CHAPTER XV

JUST A FRIEND

THE little Chaplin girls came running to meet Ellie as, smiling and full of delight over all that had happened that morning, she came into the garden. They had seen Governor Trumbull and his staff arrive at the Hinman house; but as Mrs. Chaplin had said that he was an old friend of Ellie's grandmother, they did not for a moment imagine that his visit had anything to do with their little friend. They were eager to tell Ellie of how frightened they had all been at her disappearance, and how delighted they were when Peter brought the news that she had been safe at home all night. Mildred had ventured to say that: "Perhaps Ellie went into the spare room on purpose, just to frighten her grandmother." But Bertha had instantly declared that Ellie wasn't "that kind."

"Ellie always plays fair," Bertha had said, and as the younger sisters always accepted Bertha's opinion no more was said. But Mildred wondered to herself what had happened to make Ellie look so happy as she came running to meet them.

"Oh, girls, come into the summer-house. What do you suppose I said when I woke up in the spare room this morning?" said Ellie, after they had exchanged greetings.

There was a chorus of questions. Mildred had clasped Ellie's hand, Nancy was clinging to her other arm, while Bertha and Lucy, eager and smiling, kept as near to her as possible.

"Well, I woke up and didn't know where I was," began Ellie, "and there was Grandma Hinman in the bed beside me, asleep; I *thought* she was asleep, but she wasn't. And I began to talk out loud and say: 'Oh, this is another dream. Perhaps Brownie is a dream, too. Perhaps I didn't find her picking grandma's strawberries; and perhaps I didn't ask Hannah Jane for a cake to give her'—and then grandma opened her eyes. She had heard every word, and she was so glad; because, you see, she had thought that I had eaten the strawberries and the cake. And she says I may ask Brownie to come and see me," concluded Ellie, wondering why Mildred had let go her hand, and Nancy no longer clasped her arm.

For a moment none of the girls spoke. They felt that Ellie had betrayed their secret. To do things for a little girl of whom nobody knew, to give up something they wanted in order that Brownie might have it, and keep it all unknown to grown-up people, had seemed worth while. And now Ellie had spoiled it all by telling

her grandmother. Mildred looked at Bertha a little tri-
umphantly. Was Ellie "playing fair" now? Mildred did
not believe Ellie's story. "She made that up," she
thought, and was now quite sure that her idea of Ellie
hiding in the spare room on purpose was true.

"Did you tell your grandmother *all* our secrets?"
asked Mildred scornfully; "about the 'Five Roses,'
and 'Fort Danger' and the hiding-place under the flat
stone? You could make believe that you dreamed
those, too."

Ellie's smile vanished as she listened to Mildred's
angry words, and saw that the others were looking at
her with accusing eyes. She had been so sure that they
would understand just how it had happened, and that
it was exactly as she had described.

"I truly did not mean to tell," she said slowly, looking from one to the other of her friends, hoping for some
kindly look of understanding, and then adding a little
defiantly, "but I am glad I did."

"Come, girls, we had better go home," said Mildred,
taking Lucy by the hand. "Good-bye, Miss Ellen Elizabeth Barlow," and she marched out of the summer-
house, followed by her sisters.

Ellie watched them go without a word. "I suppose
they think I did tell about Fort Danger," she thought.
Then she began to cry. It had seemed such a wonderful thing to have four little girls for neighbors—four lit-

tle girls who were ready to be friendly, and to include her in all their pleasures. And now they had deserted her. What was the use of a pretty blue India muslin and fine shoes with silver buckles, or even the praise of Governor Jonathan Trumbull, if the little Chaplin girls no longer believed and trusted her?

"Don't cry, Ellie." The soft whisper made her stop suddenly. "It was Bertha," she thought happily, "come back to make friends," and she turned about to see Brownie standing there, looking as if she too was very unhappy.

"Oh! I hoped it was Bertha!" Ellie exclaimed.

"No, it's only me," responded Brownie in so sorrowful a tone that for a moment Ellie forgot her own trouble.

"What is the matter, Brownie?" she asked.

"Why—why—you were crying," replied Brownie, as if that was enough to explain her own worry. "I don't suppose you care to tell me what made you cry?" she added, wishing that there was something that she could do or say to comfort Ellie.

"Yes, the Chaplin girls don't like me any more. I told Grandma Hinman about you, Brownie, and they don't like it."

"Oh!" Brownie drew a long breath, and looked as if she were ready to run away too. "What did your grandma say? About me, I mean?" she asked.

"She was real glad, Brownie. I don't know as she was glad about the strawberries, but she was glad that I told her. And she said I must ask you to come and see me. Where are you going?" for Brownie had started for the door.

"She'll ask me questions, and maybe have me shut up," declared Brownie in a frightened voice; but before she finished Ellie was beside her, holding her fast by the arm.

"She won't, Brownie. Truly. She is always kind, and she will smile at you and say that she is glad to see you," Ellie declared earnestly and looked up to see Grandma Hinman standing in the door of the summer-house.

"You are glad to see Brownie, are you not, grandma?" and Brownie looked up to see a kindly face smiling down at her.

"Why, of course I am. So you helped Ellie to give Governor Trumbull a message which was of the greatest importance!" she said. "I am sure the governor would wish to thank you, as he did Ellie, this very morning."

"Yes, indeed," added Ellie, who was now smiling and had quite forgotten her own trouble.

"You must stay and have dinner with Ellie," Mrs. Hinman added, but Brownie shook her head.

"Thank you, ma'am, but I mustn't stay. My father is at home, and Joe. We are going to have a dinner ourselves to-day," she added proudly. "You see, I found a golden sovereign yesterday, and so I bought some things to eat, and I got Joe some clothes, and I have five shillings left," she added with so much happiness in her voice that grandma and Ellie were both glad that she had found a golden sovereign. And Ellie resolved quickly never to let Brownie know that she had lost a sovereign.

Brownie went into the house with her friends, and Hannah Jane, after a sharp look at the little girl, smiled a little grimly; and when Brownie declared that it was time for her to go Hannah Jane stood at the door with a covered basket. "Here, lassie; the mistress put a few bits in this for ye," she said kindly, so that Brownie started for home quite sure that she had made new friends that morning.

But in spite of all her good fortune she was not quite happy. She remembered Ellie's tears. "And it was because she told about me that she was crying," thought Brownie, feeling as if she were in some way to blame.

Little Joe was on the outlook for her as usual, and came running to meet her. "A man came after father," he announced proudly, "a tall soldier man, and he gave me a shilling."

Brownie was not altogether pleased at his news. What could a soldier man want of her father? she wondered. But there was the basket to open, and dinner to prepare, and she was so excited over the meat pie and molasses cookies which the basket contained, as well as a loaf of broad, that she forgot to worry about her father.

"We'll set a table, Joe, like folks do who have dinner every day," she said proudly, drawing a rickety old table to the center of the room, and bringing her few dishes from a shelf in the corner of the room.

Before their table was spread they heard their father's step at the door, and they both ran to meet him, eager to tell of the meat pie and cookies, and of the potatoes and cabbage which Brownie had put to boil in the kettle over the fire.

"I have some good news, myself," said Mr. Vincent. "I'm to be one of the watchmen where the powder is stored. I begin this night," he concluded.

"Then we will stay here! I'm so glad," said May, looking around the dark, untidy room as if it were the most beautiful place she could imagine.

"Maybe we can fix up the place a bit," said her father. "Things seem to be improving for us. 'Tis like a miracle," he added to himself in a whisper. "Me to have steady work, and folks wishing to be kind to my girl."

Brownie was too busy at home that afternoon to go to Fort Danger for her first lesson in penmanship. It was late in the afternoon when she saw Bertha Chaplin coming down the lane toward the house.

"Why didn't you come to Fort Danger, the way you promised?" asked Bertha, as Brownie came to the door.

"I couldn't come. You know I said perhaps I couldn't," she explained. "My father has steady work now, and I'm going to keep house just the way other folks do," Brownie added proudly.

"Well, I can give you a lesson here, if you wish me to," said Bertha.

But there was not such a thing as ink, a quill pen or a scrap of paper in the poor little house.

"How were you going to teach me at Fort Danger?" questioned Brownie.

For a moment Bertha stood looking at her, then she began to laugh. "I never thought about pen and ink," she owned. "I guess you had better come to my house for a lesson, anyway. You see Ellen Barlow told her grandmother about you, and she told my grandmother. So you are not a secret any more; you are just a friend."

CHAPTER XVI

A TEA PARTY

ELLIE sewed on the muslin dress, sitting beside Grandma Hinman in the big pleasant chamber. Grandma told the little girl of the days when Ellie's mother had sat in that very chair and sewed, just as Ellie was doing, and Ellie listened eagerly. It was difficult to imagine her mother as a little girl.

"Your mother had a playhouse at the end of the garden," said grandma, "and she had two Maltese kittens for playmates. They used to follow her about everywhere."

"There is a big Maltese cat in Hannah Jane's kitchen," said Ellie.

"It is one of the great-grandchildren of your mother's kittens," said grandma smilingly, and Ellie resolved to make friends with this cat, and to ask grandma to show her where her mother's playhouse had been.

The hour passed quickly, and then Mrs. Hinman sent Ellie out to the summer-house.

"Peter will show you where your mother used to 'keep house,'" grandma said, as she folded up the work.

The day seemed very long to Ellie, and she wondered what the little Chaplin girls were doing.

"I suppose they are all at Fort Danger," she thought with a little sigh, as she walked along the path to the summer-house. Just then she felt something rub against her ankle and looked down to find the big Maltese cat close beside her; and just behind the cat ran two little Maltese kittens, so fat and round that they seemed like little balls of gray fur.

"Oh, Maltie!" exclaimed Ellie, sitting down and reaching out to take one of the kittens into her lap. "Did you bring the kittens on purpose for me to see them?" she continued, smoothing Maltie's sleek head with one hand while she held one of the kittens with the other.

Maltie purred with satisfaction. This was exactly as things ought to be, she seemed to say, as she settled down comfortably in Ellie's lap while the kittens bounced about like rubber balls, stopping now and then to look at their new playmate as if to assure her that she was quite welcome to share in their games.

Peter, coming along the path, smiled down on the little group. "Weel! Weel!" he said. "'Tis like the days when your mither was a little lass playing in this garden."

"Where was her playhouse, Peter? Will you please show me?" Ellie asked, jumping up, but still holding the two kittens in her arms.

"Yes, indeed, Miss Ellen, and 'tis a pity ye have not been there before," said Peter, leading the way along the path, closely followed by Ellie and Maltie.

"'Tis at the far end of the garden behind the lilacs," said Peter. "There's a small bench there I made for your mither, but there's not much else the same."

It was a pleasant shady corner, and Ellie looked about and wished that her mother was there beside her as she sat down on the little bench. She looked up to thank Peter, but he had turned back to the house. But the kittens proved good playmates, and Ellie was trying to think what names she should give them, when a rustling noise made her look up, and there stood Hannah Jane carrying a basket, and smiling as Ellie had never seen Hannah Jane smile before.

"I've been hoping ye'd come to this corner, Miss Ellie," she said, resting the basket on the bench beside the little girl, "and what do ye call the kittens?"

"I was trying to think of names. What did my mother call her kittens?"

"To think of your wantin' to know that! Weel, I can tell ye. Your mither always called her little cats Rosy and Posy," said Hannah Jane, who was now taking the cover from the basket.

Ellie laughed happily. "Then I'll call my kittens Rosy and Posy. I can call the kittens mine while I stay, can't I, Hannah Jane?"

"To be sure ye can. An' I doubt not ye can take them home with ye, if so be ye want to," responded Hannah

Jane, who now regarded Ellie with great kindness, and no longer called her "Miss Ellen Elizabeth."

"Look at this now, Miss Ellie," and Ellie looked up to see Hannah Jane holding a tiny cup and saucer in each hand. She set them down on the bench beside the little girl, with a word of warning to the "little cats," and in a few moments there was an entire little tea-set of sprigged china on the bench beside Ellie.

"Your grandmither has been saving these all the past years to give ye when you came here for a visit," explained Hannah Jane, "an' now I'll fetch the little round table and ye can ask the little girls next door to a tea party."

"I—I—I'd rather have just grandma, Hannah Jane," Ellie replied, greatly to Hannah Jane's approval.

There were other things beside the tea-set in the basket. There were six tiny silver spoons, and six small damask napkins, and in one corner of the basket there was a doll. A china doll, with red cheeks, and black eyes, and wearing a scarlet dress, and shoes of scarlet silk.

Ellie lifted it out very carefully. Old Maltie was asleep on the grass with Rosy and Posy running about. For the moment Ellie quite forgot them as she sat holding this beautiful doll, and looking at the sprigged china; and when Hannah Jane returned with the little round table s she aid: "Your grandmither and Mrs. Ludlow are coming to take tea with ye. I'll step back to the house and fetch the tray. The doll's name is Angeline."

"'Angeline,' 'Rosy' and 'Posy.'" Ellie repeated the names of her new friends with delight, and when Grandma Hinman and Mrs. Ludlow arrived they found a very happy and smiling little girl ready to greet them.

Ellie did not forget her curtsy this time, and Mrs. Ludlow, just lifting her skirts with her finger-tips, made a deep curtsy in response, with the gay little laugh which had so delighted Ellie on their first meeting in the stage-coach.

Then Hannah Jane came round the big lilac tree with the tray. Ellie spread the little table and served her guests, not forgetting to set a saucer of cream for Rosy and Posy, and to urge Angeline to help herself to the cake.

Mrs. Ludlow was greatly interested to hear the story of the young English deserter from the British Army.

"I make no doubt but what many of the English soldiers will stay in this country at the end of the war, and be ready to defend America when need be," she said. "And we can ask for no better citizens than those of English blood."

Ellie looked at Mrs. Ludlow in surprise, for it was a time when loyal Americans had but few words of praise for the English; but the good lady nodded and said:

"Your own grandfather was as fine an Englishman as the best, Miss Ellen. And the English must suffer now because of the pride and folly of their Tory king."

"Yes, ma'am," responded Ellie, so promptly that both the ladies laughed.

"I have been telling my little granddaughters some old English riddles," continued Mrs. Ludlow. "Now I'll see if you can guess one:

> "'There was a girl in our town,
>   Silk *an*' satin was her gown,
>   Silk *an*' satin, gold *an*' velvet,
>   Guess her name, three times I've telled it.'"

But Ellie could not guess it.

"Ann," said Mrs. Ludlow, with her gay laugh.

"Tell me another!" urged Ellie.

"Well, here is one that I am sure you will guess," agreed Mrs. Ludlow.

> "'Flour of England, fruit of Spain,
>   Met together in a shower of rain;
>   Put in a bag tied round with a string,
>   If you'll tell me this riddle I'll give you a ring.'"

But Ellie shook her head hopelessly, and when Mrs. Ludlow said: "A plum-pudding, of course," she wondered why she had not thought of it at once.

"Do you know any riddles, grandma?" asked Ellie.

"No, dear child. I cannot remember one, I am sorry to say," responded Mrs. Hinman. "When Hannah Jane comes for the tray ask her to tell you some of the old proverbs that she so often quotes."

"What is a 'proverb'?" asked Ellie, who had never before heard the word.

"I suppose it is what Hannah Jane would call 'a wise saying,'" replied Mrs. Hinman.

It was not long before Hannah Jane appeared, and Ellie ran to meet her.

"Hannah Jane, would you please to tell me a proverb?" she asked.

"Yes, Hannah Jane," said Mrs. Hinman. "You know you taught Ellie's mother a number of useful proverbs."

The old Scotchwoman was evidently pleased at the suggestion. Looking straight over Ellie's head, and speaking each word very distinctly, she repeated:

> " 'For every evil under the sun,
>   There be a remedy, or there be none.
>   If there be one, try and find it;
>   If there be none, never mind it.'"

"Oh, I have heard my mother say that," declared Ellie.

"Weel, 'twas mesilf taught her the words," said Hannah Jane, bearing away the tray.

"I came on an errand, and I have been so well entertained that I nearly forgot it," said Mrs. Ludlow, as she rose to go. "Mr. and Mrs. Chaplin bade me ask if Mrs. Hinman and Ellie would do them the honor of being their guests on a picnic to the Charter Oak on Thursday. We plan to go in the big wagon."

"Yes, indeed," Mrs. Hinman replied. "It is most kind of Mrs. Chaplin, and I am very glad that Ellie can see the place where Connecticut's charter was safely hidden."

Neither of the older ladies thought it strange that Ellie should remain silent. It was considered only proper that children should not speak on such occasions, unless asked to do so; and Mrs. Hinman and Mrs. Ludlow were both sure that Ellie must be pleased at the thought of the proposed excursion with her young friends.

"Thank you, grandma, for letting me play with the tea-set and the doll," said Ellie, putting Angeline carefully back in the corner of the basket.

"But, dear child, you can play with them whenever you please. They are yours. I meant to give them to you as soon as you came, but the days have passed so quickly that I nearly forgot," responded grandma.

"It seems as if I had everything," declared Ellie, holding Angeline very closely, and looking at the two kittens. "I wish my mother could see us this minute. I guess she would be glad."

"Now I will tell you what I plan to do with the kittens," said grandma, lifting "Posy" to her lap. "I plan for you to take them home when you go, as a present to your mother."

"It's been lovely this afternoon, grandma. I have had the best time of all my visit," said Ellie, for she was resolved to remember Hannah Jane's proverb, and not be unhappy over the desertion of the little Chaplin girls. For she knew that she had not deserved their unkindness. And as she could not find any way to remedy the trouble she resolved "not to mind it," and carrying Angeline in her arms, with Rosy and Posy bouncing along beside her, she walked back to the house with her grandmother, listening attentively to Mrs. Hinman's story of Angeline, who had been purchased in London by a seafaring relative of Ellie's grandfather, and brought home as a present to Mr. Hinman's little daughter.

CHAPTER XVII

MILDRED AND NANCY

It was the day after Ellie's tea party in the garden, and the little Chaplin girls were all at Fort Danger; but they were not in their usual good spirits.

Brownie had come to the house for her first lesson in writing, but she had been very quiet, and had hurried away to join Ellie in Mrs. Hinman's summer-house. The Chaplin girls had heard from Mrs. Ludlow all about the wonderful tea-set, the doll, and the two Maltese kittens, and Lucy had cried because her sisters would not let her go and play with Ellie and see all these delightful things. If Mildred had not constantly reminded her sisters that Ellie was a "traitor," in having betrayed a secret which was not wholly her own, Nancy and Bertha would have agreed to let Lucy carry out her plan, and perhaps have gone with her.

That very morning Mrs. Ludlow had praised Ellie very highly, speaking of her pretty manners and her good disposition, and even praising her for telling Mrs. Hinman about May Vincent. "Although of course Ellie did not realize that she was awake," Mrs. Ludlow had said. The sisters were thinking of what their grandmother had said as they reached the fort.

"What are we going to play to-day?" asked Nancy. "Shall we play General Washington and Lafayette? If we do, I'm going to be Lafayette," and she looked questioningly toward Bertha.

But Bertha shook her head. "No," she replied. "I have been thinking about Ellen Barlow, and I think we weren't fair. It was horrid to speak to her the way you did, Mildred. And I have made up my mind to go straight back and tell her that I am sorry," and Bertha approached the edge of the terrace ready to slide down.

"Oh, goody!" exclaimed Lucy. "I'll go, too."

"And so will I," said Nancy. "Come on, Mildred. You ought to be the first one to tell Ellie that you are sorry, for you really made all the trouble."

"Take that back, Nancy Chaplin," exclaimed Mildred, Springing up, her face flushed with anger. "Just because I was honest and spoke the truth, you put all the blame on me. All you want to make up with her for is so that you can play with her tea-set and that old doll."

Bertha and Lucy had already slid down the bank and started for home, expecting the others would quickly follow. They had not heard Mildred's angry words.

"I won't take it back," Nancy replied valiantly. "You just the same as told Ellie that she had spoken a falsehood. And you know she told the truth. You can stay here and sulk if you want to. I've a great mind to tell mother all about it," and Nancy turned to follow her sisters.

But Mildred was now too angry to realize what she was doing. She ran toward her sister and gave her an ugly push, which sent poor little Nancy tumbling headlong over the steep cliff. Nancy screamed as she felt herself going, and Bertha looked back quickly, just in time to see her little sister as she fell in the grass beneath the fort.

Bertha ran back as fast as she could go. Nancy was lying there in a little huddled heap, apparently stunned by the fall.

"Run and fill your hat with water, Lucy," said Bertha as she straightened out the little figure. "Oh, Nancy, how did you happen to fall?" she whispered.

In a moment Lucy was back with her pretty hat dripping with water, and as Bertha turned it over Nancy's face she moved slightly and opened her eyes. Then she moaned as if in pain.

"My arm hurts," she said faintly, "and so does my foot."

"Mildred! Mildred!" called Bertha. "Come down. Nancy is hurt," and as Mildred, with white face and frightened eyes stood beside them, Bertha said: "Hurry! Run just as fast as you can, and tell mother that Nancy fell off the fort and is hurt;" and Mildred raced off, while Bertha lifted Nancy to a sitting position and let her rest against her shoulder, while she endeavored to comfort her. It was evident that Nancy was in great pain, but she was trying to be brave.

Lucy sat close by. "I think Nancy is brave," she said, and Nancy responded with a little whisper: "Five Roses," which made Bertha take courage.

As Mildred raced along the path toward home the tears were running down her cheeks.

"What shall I do? What shall I do?" she sobbed aloud, wishing with all her heart that she had not given Nancy that angry push. When she came rushing into the house her mother exclaimed in fright at her little daughter's woeful appearance.

"It's Nancy! She is hurt. Oh, hurry," cried Mildred, "down at the foot of the bluff. She can't walk," and almost before she had finished speaking Mrs. Chaplin had started, while Mrs. Ludlow questioned Mildred, and decided that it would be best to send the gardener to bring Nancy home, and to ask Mrs. Hinman to send Peter for a physician.

Mildred had thrown herself on a wide settle in the sitting-room. She heard them when they brought Nancy home and carried her up-stairs. She heard the doctor's arrival, and then she got up and crept to the stairway. A dreadful fear had entered her heart. Suppose that Nancy should always be lame?

"The doctor will know," she thought, and resolved to wait until he came down the stairs and ask him.

"Don't feel so bad, Mildred," and a kindly arm was about her shoulder and Bertha stood beside her. "The doctor says that her ankle is only sprained."

"Will she ever walk?" whispered Mildred.

"Yes, indeed; very soon. But her poor little arm is broken. Oh, Mildred!" for Mildred had begun to sob so bitterly that Bertha could not comfort her.

Ellie and Brownie soon heard the news of Nancy's mishap, and when Brownie started for home Mrs. Hinman suggested that Ellie should go in to Mrs. Chaplin's to inquire what the doctor had said.

Ellie agreed without a word. But as she went up the path to the Chaplin house she wondered what Bertha and Mildred would do if they saw her coming to their house. She did not have long to wonder, for Lucy came running to meet her, closely followed by Bertha.

They were eager to tell her about Nancy's accident, for no one imagined that it was Mildred's fault which had caused her fall.

"And we were just starting to go to your house, Ellie. We wanted to ask your pardon," said Bertha.

"Five Roses," responded Ellie. "I don't believe the 'Roses' need to ask each other's pardon. But truly, I did not mean to tell. And I did not say a word about Fort Danger or the 'Roses.'"

"We are all glad that your grandma knows about Brownie," said Bertha, "and I'm glad we are friends again. It was horrid to feel that we had been mean to you."

"Where is Mildred?" asked Lucy. "I haven't seen her since the doctor went."

"She has cried herself nearly sick about Nancy," said Bertha, "but Nancy will soon be able to come downstairs, and then you must come and see her, Ellie."

Ellie was glad to promise to come, and when Bertha slipped her hand under Ellie's arm in the old friendly fashion and walked home with her, telling of Nancy's scream and of running back to find her little sister unconscious, she could not help but feel happy in spite of the sad accident.

"Mildred feels awfully," said Bertha. "I never knew her to cry so much as she has about Nancy. And mother has forbidden us ever to go near Fort Danger again. You see, we had to tell how we happened to be there, and now we haven't a secret left, only the 'Five Roses,'" concluded Bertha a little apologetically, for she had suddenly realized that it was not always possible to keep a secret.

"I think the 'Roses' is the best of all, don't you, Bertha?" Ellie responded; "and if you want to tell your mother about that it will be all right."

Bertha shook her head. "No," she answered quickly, "let's not tell that."

From an upper window Mildred had watched Ellie's arrival, and had seen Bertha and Lucy run to meet her.

"I suppose they will tell her it was all my fault that we treated her badly; and it was. I was to blame for that, and now I have nearly killed Nancy," thought the unhappy child.

She knew that Nancy was suffering, and that no one but her mother was to enter her room until the next day. She wondered if Nancy had told that it was she, Mildred, who had given the angry push which had sent Nancy over the steep bluff?

"If she hasn't told already she will tell to-morrow. Perhaps she is waiting to tell father," decided Mildred. That her father should know that she had been angry enough to do such a thing seemed all the punishment she could bear. She was sure that her father, mother and sisters could never again care for her when they discovered that she was to blame for Nancy's broken arm.

"What shall I do?" she sobbed aloud, not knowing that Mrs. Ludlow had just entered the room.

"Why, dear Mildred, what is the matter?" asked her grandmother, putting her arm about the unhappy child. "Can't you tell grandma?"

"I pushed Nancy. I pushed her off the fort," sobbed the little girl.

"But you did not mean to; it was an accident," said Mrs. Ludlow.

"I didn't mean to hurt her. But I was angry—" Mildred stopped suddenly. What had she done? she thought, thoroughly frightened. She had told Grandma Ludlow something that she had feared for any one to know.

"Oh, grandma! I didn't mean to tell!" she said pleadingly, looking up into Mrs. Ludlow's kind face.

"I will never speak of it, my child, unless you ask me to," responded her grandmother, "but I am sure you will decide that you want your mother to know. It is a very serious and unhappy thing for you to have such a secret. The only way to overcome your trouble, dear child, is to tell Nancy how sorry you are—"

"Yes, yes; I will," interrupted Mildred eagerly. "I mean to."

"And tell your mother and father at once," concluded Mrs. Ludlow.

CHAPTER XVIII

HANNAH JANE AND ELLIE

THE day after Nancy's accident Ellie received a letter from her mother, saying that her father had joined his regiment, which had been sent to defend the Northern frontier. She spoke of "Barlay," and said that they were now quite sure that he must be a relative, and that the boys called him "cousin."

"You must tell your grandmother about him," Mrs. Barlow had written to her little daughter; "very soon now you will be coming home, and then I will tell you about Barlay."

Mrs. Hinman read the letter with interest.

"I have no doubt but the young Englishman awoke to the fact that the rights of a slave may be invaded without protest, but that no loyal subject will yield without a hearing, and the English king refuses to hear us," she said.

"If the charter granted to Connecticut by King Charles in 1662 could be read by all British soldiers, 'twould end the war," she added, for all Connecticut people firmly believed that their charter was a model form of government.

"Was that the charter which was hid in the oak?" asked Ellie.

"Yes, my dear, and that reminds me that of course our excursion with the Chaplins will have to be postponed until little Nancy is better," said Mrs. Hinman, "and it may be they will think best to give it up altogether."

While Mrs. Hinman was speaking Hannah Jane had entered the room, and stood waiting.

"If you please, ma'am, I've been a-thinking of the little Vincent lass an' her brither," she began; "it seems there's no woman-folk to do a hand's turn for the children. An' Peter has been down for a look at the place, an' says 'tis little better than a shed." And Hannah Jane stood as if waiting for some suggestion from her mistress.

"And what can we do about it, Hannah Jane?" responded Mrs. Hinman.

"Weel, ma'am, Peter was saying that if ye would spare him this afternoon he'd weel like to step down an' mend the floor an' the windows fer the children. An', if ye please, ma'am, I could go down mesilf and help the lassie a bit," said Hannah Jane.

"Couldn't I go too, grandma?" asked Ellie, taking it for granted that her grandmother would instantly approve of this plan. But Mrs. Hinman's look was troubled.

"We must not forget that May and Joe have a father. He might think ill of our interference," she said.

"I nigh forgot, ma'am. Peter made the acquaintance of their faither, and Mr. Vincent is weel pleased at the idea," said Hannah Jane, and now Mrs. Hinman smiled.

"I see it is all settled," she said, "and if Hannah Jane is willing to take you, Ellie, you may go with her to see May Vincent."

"To be sure Miss Ellie may go. We'll be starting right away after dinner, ma'am," responded Hannah Jane briskly.

"I'll sew my hour this morning," said Ellie. "I am sure to finish the long seams to-day."

Grandma nodded approvingly, and Ellie ran upstairs and got out her work-bag and sat down to work on her dress. She wondered if Rosy and Posy, followed by their careful mother, were running about the garden, and she thought of Angeline, in her beautiful scarlet dress, who was now sitting in one of the chairs in Ellie's own room.

"If Nancy had not broken her arm there would not be a single unhappy thing, not one!" the little girl thought happily, remembering with delight that the little Chaplin girls were again her friends.

At that moment she heard a little tap on the door, and heard some one say:

"Your grandma told me to come up, but if you don't want to speak to me I'll go right home," and Ellie looked up to see Mildred standing just inside the door.

"Oh, Mildred! I'm so glad to see you. Is Nancy better?" exclaimed Ellie, jumping up from her chair, and starting toward her friend.

"Wait, Ellie, I've got to tell you something dreadful. I am to blame about Nancy. Yes, I am. And it all came because I was mean and hateful to you," said Mildred, still keeping close to the door, as if sure that Ellie would not want her to stay when she heard what Mildred knew she must tell her. She spoke quickly, saying that her sisters had been sure of Ellie's truth, and that she, Mildred, had been so angry at Nancy's determination to make friends that she had given her the push which sent the poor child over the cliff.

"And if you can't forgive me I sha'n't blame you a bit," Mildred said as she finished.

Ellie stood listening as if she could hardly understand what Mildred had told her, and Mildred went on: "I have told mother and father, and Nancy has forgiven me. But Bertha says she's so ashamed of me that she can hardly bear to look at me," and now Mildred sobbed aloud, for the younger girls all thought that Bertha was exactly right in whatever she decided to do, and Bertha's disapproval was hard for Mildred to bear.

"Well, Mildred! I think you are splendid!" declared Ellie, coming close to her friend. "Anybody gets angry; and of course you wouldn't have hurt Nancy on purpose, but it's a true deed to do all you have done to make it right."

Mildred's face brightened, but she shook her head. Not only Grandma Ludlow but her mother and father had talked to her so seriously about the dangers of an ill-controlled temper that Mildred was sure she would never again dare to be angry. She could not forget that Nancy must suffer because of that ugly moment when her sister had forgotten everything because she could not have her own way.

"I did think of the vow of the Five Roses when I told father," Mildred acknowledged, "and I want to tell you something else: Bertha said that I must apologize to you, and I do."

Ellie leaned forward and kissed Mildred's flushed cheek. "Come and see Angeline," she said, "and then I'll show you Rosy and Posy," and hand in hand the two girls went down the hall to Ellie's room, where Mildred admired Angeline and for the moment forgot her trouble.

"Now you must see Rosy and Posy," said Ellie, and Mildred followed Ellie to the kitchen to be welcomed pleasantly by Hannah Jane.

Taking the kittens the girls went out to the playhouse under the lilacs.

"I must not stay long," said Mildred, "because Nancy may need me. Bertha is reading to her now, but I am to do everything I can for her. Mother said that I might."

"When will she come down-stairs?" asked Ellie.

"AREN'T YOU GOING TO STAY ALL SUMMER?"

"In a day or two. Her ankle is better to-day. And her arm is in a sling," said Mildred in so mournful a tone that Ellie began to talk about the tea party which she meant to have in the playhouse as soon as Nancy could come: "That is, if she is well enough to come to a tea party before I go home. You see, my visit is half finished."

"Oh! Aren't you going to stay all summer? I thought you were," responded Mildred.

"I couldn't do that," replied Ellie, "but I shall miss you all. It's lovely to have girls for neighbors," and she told Mildred about her home, and its distance from school and neighbors.

Mildred looked much happier when she started for home than on her arrival at Ellie's, and Ellie returned to her sewing, and finished her stent before dinner.

"May I not wipe the dishes for you to-day, Hannah Jane?" she asked, when dinner was over, and Hannah Jane was clearing the table.

"'Tis for your grandma to say," replied Hannah Jane.

"Of course you may. Tie an apron over your frock," replied Mrs. Hinman, smiling with approval at Ellie's suggestion; and Ellie remembered that her mother had said it would be a great favor if Hannah Jane allowed her to help with the household work.

It was evident that Hannah Jane was glad of her assistance, and as Ellie carefully wiped the dishes and set them away, Hannah Jane told her of her plan to help the Vincents to make their home more comfortable.

"The lass is a good lass," she declared, as she spoke of Brownie; "she spent the gold piece she found on things for her brither, and a bit of food; na' penny's worth did she buy for herself."

Ellie made no response to this. She was quite sure that the sovereign Brownie had found was the one Barlay had given her, which she had lost. Brownie had found it near the fence under which they crawled, and Ellie thought it had probably slipped from her pocket. But she did not even let Brownie know of her loss, nor did she again speak to her grandmother about it. It had seemed a wonderful sum to Ellie; she had planned to buy a beautiful bead purse for her mother, and gifts for all the family; but as soon as she realized that Brownie had found it she said to herself that she would keep her vow to the "Five Roses," and never let Brownie know of her own loss.

"It isn't really much of a 'true deed,'" she owned to herself, "but it's something." So Ellie no longer thought of the lost money. Her mother would be as well pleased, she knew, with the two Maltese kittens as with any gift Ellie could bring.

"Your grandma is sending a braided rug, a couple of chairs and some dishes to the Vincents. Peter will take the things on his wheelbarrow," said Hannah Jane, as she and Ellie started for Brown Lane.

Brownie was at the Chaplins' for her daily lesson, and when she reached home she looked about in surprise.

Peter was at work on the roof, and had already mended the kitchen floor, which Hannah Jane had thoroughly swept and scrubbed. The braided rug lay in the centre of the room, the two chairs stood near the table, the windows had been washed, and Hannah Jane was now putting up some curtains of figured chintz, while Ellie was setting the dishes Mrs. Hinman had sent on the dresser shelves.

"Are you surprised, Brownie?" Ellie asked, smiling with delight at Brownie's happy face.

"I was thinking about Joe. I don't know what he will say," said Brownie; "father took him to help guard the powder this afternoon. I guess I never can thank you," and she turned to Hannah Jane, as if quite sure that Hannah Jane understood all she could not say.

When Hannah Jane had finished an afternoon of hard work, the three rooms of the old cabin were clean and fresh, and it seemed a very different place from the cabin of Ellie's first visit. Brownie danced about from room to room looking admiringly at the pretty patchwork quilt which Hannah Jane had spread over Brownie's narrow cot, and then at the neat kitchen.

"It's just like a home, isn't it?" she said to Ellie, "and we won't move. Father says that we won't. I never expected to have so much." Then she looked at Ellie earnestly. "And it's all because you were kind," she said; "if you had driven me away that day when you found me in your grandma's garden—" and Brownie choked a little, and said no more; but Ellie understood, and was as glad as Brownie herself that she had been kind to her.

"Come up to-morrow and see my playhouse," said Ellie as she bade Brownie good-bye and ran after Hannah Jane.

"Hannah Jane," she said, reaching up to clasp her friend's hand, "you know you said it well became any little girl to think about other children?"

"Did I now, Miss Ellie? Weel, to be sure, maybe I did," responded Hannah Jane.

"Yes, Hannah Jane. 'Twas when I cried about spoiling my hat," Ellie reminded her, "and I want to tell you that I think I know what you meant. You meant it makes any one happy to make other people happy."

Hannah Jane smiled down at the eager little face, and her clasp on Ellie's hand tightened.

"Maybe that's what I did mean, and knew naught of it, Miss Ellie," she replied.

CHAPTER XIX

THE END OF THE VISIT

IT was several days before Nancy came down-stairs, and Ellie was her first visitor. The two friends had many things to talk about, and Ellie had brought Angeline for Nancy to see and admire.

"Mildred does everything for me," Nancy declared proudly. "Grandma Ludlow says that she is my 'lady in waiting,' such as queens have."

Mildred flushed a little at her sister's praise. It was evident that Nancy had quite forgiven her sister for the ugly push, and for the suffering it had brought.

"I hope you can come over and see my tea-set and the Maltese kittens before I go home," said Ellie. "I am going next week."

"Next week!" exclaimed Nancy in surprise. "Oh, Ellie! we don't want you to go. Why can't you stay and live with your grandma?" But Ellie shook her head smilingly.

"It's lovely to be going home. *You* wouldn't care to stay away from home, no matter how good a time you were having; and I have had a good time," responded

Ellie, "and the very best part of it all has been having you girls for neighbors," she added.

"Here comes Bertha," said Mildred, from her seat near the window; "she has something for you and for Nancy," and Mildred tried to look as if she were keeping a great secret.

"What is it, Mildred?" Nancy asked eagerly; but before Mildred could reply Bertha entered the room, closely followed by Lucy.

"What is the secret, Bertha?" questioned Nancy.

"Secret?" said Bertha in surprise. "Why, I haven't any secret! Oh, you mean the 'Roses.'"

"No, I don't. What is it you have for Ellie and me?" said Nancy.

"Why, the 'Roses,'" repeated Bertha. "You know we vowed to each wear a rose as an emblem of our vows. And then Ellie discovered Brownie, and so many things began to happen that we forgot all about it."

"So we did," agreed Ellie.

"Well, I remembered it yesterday, and so I made five tiny roses out of white silk. Lucy, will you please run up-stairs to my room and bring me my work-bag?" and Lucy started off instantly and was back in a moment with the pretty bag of flowered chintz.

Bertha opened it and took out the five tiny roses and laid them on Nancy's lap.

"They look like buttons!" declared Mildred, "but they are pretty," she added quickly.

Bertha did not make any reply. She had worked all the morning to make the tiny "roses," and she had hoped that her sisters and Ellie would think that she had done well. After a moment she smiled and said: "Well, we can call them roses, can't we? And even if they do look like 'buttons' they will remind us of each other," and she pinned one on Ellie's dress, and handed another to Mildred.

Mildred's face had flushed, and now she spoke quickly: "Nobody but me would have said such a hateful thing, Bertha. I'm sorry."

"You need not be sorry a bit. They do look like buttons," replied Bertha, with a friendly nod to Mildred, but the elder sister was thinking to herself how different this was from the "old Mildred." A week ago and Mildred would never have owned a mistake, or asked pardon for anything. Poor Nancy's tumble seemed to have made Mildred realize that she must consider the feelings of others.

Mildred pinned the "rose" on Nancy's dress, and each of the girls thought they would always treasure this little remembrance of Fort Danger and their promises to each other. Ellie had just said that it was time for her to go home whenMrs. Ludlow came hurrying into the room. She had a newspaper in one hand, and looked as if she had just heard the best of good news.

"Here is news of the most wonderful thing which has yet been accomplished in America. A Matchless Document prepared by Congress, The Declaration of Independence," and Mrs. Ludlow looked at the little girls as if she quite expected them to understand all that such news meant to every loyal American.

"But Governor Trumbull declared our independence on the fourteenth of June," said Bertha, who recalled that her father had told her that June fourteenth was an important day in the history of Connecticut liberty.

"To be sure," agreed Mrs. Ludlow. "Connecticut has never been obliged to wait for any other Colony to lead her to freedom, but now the Thirteen Colonies are united under an American government, and we may hope for the protection of freedom. Your father will read you this paper to-night."

"Is it as wonderful as the charter of Connecticut?" asked Ellie.

"My child! It is the most sublime creation possible," replied Mrs. Ludlow. "All the town is reading it. People are marching about the streets shouting with joy; and every one declares it will inspire our soldiers to even greater deeds of valor."

Ellie thought of all that Mrs. Ludlow had said as she walked home. If this new Declaration was so wonderful, why, then America would soon be at peace; her father could stay at home, and there would be no more suffering. She wondered if her mother and brothers had heard the great news, or if she would be the first to tell them?

In a few days more Nancy, with the help of Mildred, was able to hobble over to Mrs. Hinman's garden, and to make the acquaintance of Rosy and Posy. The little tea-table was set in the summer-house on Nancy's account; and each one of the girls was eager to be of use to Nancy. Mildred was on one side and Brownie on the other, and Nancy seemed the very happiest one of the happy little group.

As Ellie looked about at the beautiful garden, and then at her friends gathered about the round table she grew very quiet. She was thinking how she would miss them all, even if she was going home, and wished that her mother might have just such a garden and summer-house as this.

"I wish that you were all going home with me," she said, looking across the table at Nancy. "Perhaps when your grandmother returns to Albany you can all come and visit me?"

"Not all of us at one time!" said Bertha, "but I shouldn't wonder if one of us could visit you then. Grandma Ludlow is going to drive you out to see the

Charter Oak to-morrow. She says she promised when you met in the coach, and now that mother has given up the picnic she means to take you herself."

This was good news to Ellie. She had been greatly disappointed at the thought of not seeing the tree on the Wyllis farm, where the old charter had been concealed, and to drive out with Mrs. Ludlow would be almost better than the proposed picnic, she thought, and Mrs. Hinman was greatly pleased at Mrs. Ludlow's friendly suggestion.

"We will take a bite of luncheon and not hurry back," Mrs. Ludlow said, when she came out to the arbor with Mrs. Hinman to tell Ellie of the plan. The other little girls looked a little sober, for they had all hoped for a picnic, and Mildred again reproached herself for bringing them this disappointment.

"If I hadn't been so hateful we could have had the picnic just as mother planned," she thought.

"It's just like being grown up," said Ellie, as she took her seat in the chaise beside Mrs. Ludlow the next morning; and Mrs. Ludlow laughed and nodded, and said, "Go on, Doll," to the fat white horse, and they were off, leaving Grandma Hinman waving her hand from the high porch.

As they drove along Ellie said to herself that she felt just as if she were grown up. "Just like Miss Ellen Elizabeth Barlow," and suddenly she looked up and said, "I'm making believe that we are both young ladies."

"That is a fine idea. I'll make believe too," declared Mrs. Ludlow; "let's be eighteen," and Ellie agreed that eighteen must be grown up enough for any one.

It was a happy day for both the elderly woman and the little girl. Their "make believe" lasted until they came driving back in the late afternoon, and Mrs. Ludlow said good-bye, and added: "It's so pleasant to have a friend of my own age," and Ellie responded:

"Yes, indeed! That's just what I think."

There were only three days more after this before Ellie's visit would be over. The little leather trunk stood in her chamber ready to be packed for the journey, and Peter was making a box, with narrow openings on the top and sides, in which Rosy and Posy could travel comfortably.

Every day there were tea parties in the summerhouse, or in the Chaplin garden under the big elms. Brownie, looking very sober indeed whenever Ellie's going home was spoken of, came every day; and every day Hannah Jane's gingerbread cakes seemed to grow larger and sweeter, and then the morning came when Ellie opened her eyes and realized that before night she would see her dear mother.

It was hard to say good-bye to Grandma Hinman, to Hannah Jane and Peter. The other good-byes had been said on the previous night, for Mrs. Chaplin knew that Mrs. Hinman would wish to have Ellie to herself on that last morning.

The little trunk stood by the gate, and on it rested the bandbox. Mr. Pettigrew drove up in grand fashion, and while Peter lifted the box containing Rosy and Posy to the back of the coach, and put the trunk in a safe place, Mr. Pettigrew leaned down and said: "I hope you have had a pleasant visit, Miss Ellen Elizabeth," and Ellie thought again how nice it was to have a name with such a really grown-up sound.

"Do you wish your bandbox in the coach, Miss Ellie?" asked Peter.

"Yes, thank you," said Ellie carelessly, holding her grandmother's hand very tightly, and not caring at all where the bandbox was put. For there was nothing in it except her hat of blue shirred silk. There was no mysterious package in the bandbox now.

CHAPTER XX

HOME AGAIN

MR. PETTIGREW waved his whip, the horses started forward at a good pace, and Ellie leaned from the coach window until a turn in the road shut out Market Square from view. Then she looked rather shyly at her traveling companions. There was no pleasant elderly woman beside her on this return journey. She had the back seat quite to herself. There were three men on the middle seat. It seemed to Ellie that they were all talking at once, and all talking of Governor Trumbull. Ellie did not mean to listen, but it was soon evident that the men were quite willing that any one should hear what they had to say. Suddenly she realized that they were discussing a mysterious letter which Governor Trumbull had received a few weeks earlier.

"'Tis said the letter was handed him on the street by a small girl," declared one of the men, "and that it came none too soon. There was a plot on foot to carry the governor off."

Ellie knew that her face was flushed. What would those men say, she wondered, if they knew that the lit-

178

tle girl who had given Governor Trumbull the letter was on the seat behind them? This would be something more to tell her mother and brothers.

The men were going to Salisbury. Their talk was soon of the Salisbury iron mines, and its foundries where cannon were cast for the use of the American army; and Ellie heard no further mention of the mysterious little girl who had given the letter to Governor Trumbull. There were other passengers on the front seat of the coach, but there was no one for Ellie to speak to. She began to wish that the box with Rosy and Posy could be put on the seat beside her, and resolved when the coach stopped at the inn to change horses that she would ask Mr. Pettigrew if this might be done.

Mr. Pettigrew came to the coach door as soon as he climbed down from his high seat.

"I hope you are enjoying your journey, Miss Ellen Elizabeth," he said; and when Ellie thanked him, and told him about Rosy and Posy, he said at once that the box could be set on the floor of the coach beside her.

"You see, they will enjoy it more if they are with me," Ellie explained, and Mr. Pettigrew smiled and nodded, and called the guard to bring "the box of cats," and in a few moments there were Rosy and Posy trying their best to get their heads through the openings in the box, and evidently delighted to be near Ellie. As she looked down at the kittens Ellie remembered her lost sovereign; and then she thought of Brownie and Joe, now well-clothed and happy; and of Hannah Jane, who had said that she meant to look after Brownie, "for your sake, Miss Ellie, since 'tis you she has to thank for all her good fortune;" and then the guard's bugle call, longer and louder than before, made Ellie look from the window.

"Oh, it's the top of Long Hill. I can see our house," she exclaimed happily, and at the sound of her voice the men on the seat turned and smiled at her.

"Why, you are a brave little miss indeed to journey from Hartford alone," said one of them.

"Did you hear of the little maid who brought a note to our governor?" questioned his companion, looking at Ellie.

"Yes, sir," Ellie replied, but she was not thinking of Hartford now, or of any of the wonderful things which had happened there. She could see her mother and brothers at the roadside waiting for her. How slowly Mr. Pettigrew was driving, she thought impatiently. And now the very best moment of all her visit was close at hand, for the coach had stopped, the door opened, and Ellie was held tight in her mother's arms.

The little leather trunk, the bandbox and "the box of cats" were set down. Mrs. Barlow thanked Mr. Pettigrew for bringing Ellie safely home; the men in the coach lifted their hats to the little group by the gate, and off went the four horses.

"Oh, mother, I have so much to tell you," said Ellie, as they turned toward the house. "And grandma sent the kittens to you. Their names are Rosy and Posy."

"Of course," replied Mrs. Barlow smilingly.

"And grandma is going to send Will a lot of silkworms; and there is a fine book in my trunk for Stevie," continued Ellie, and then she heard all the messages that her father had left for her.

Ellie ran about the house from room to room, "as if you had been away a year," declared Will laughingly.

"I do believe you have forgotten all about Barlay," said Stephen a little reproachfully, as the family gathered about the table. "You haven't even asked about him. And he worked nearly a week to make—" but Steve stopped suddenly.

"Oh, I did forget," replied Ellie, "but where is he?"

"Gone to Lebanon," said Stephen. "Governor Trumbull sent for him last week."

"Isn't he ever coming back?" asked Ellie.

"Of course he will," said Will. "He hasn't any home except with us. He's coming back to help with the harvest."

And then Mrs. Barlow told Ellie of the messenger who had brought the friendly summons for the young

Englishman. "Of course the governor wanted to see and question him," said Ellie's mother, "but we feel sure that he will come back to us."

"You haven't even looked at the orchard," Will said as Ellie went to look at her yellow rose-bush. "Come on, you'll be surprised," and Ellie ran along beside her brother to the corner of the house. Then she stopped and looked about as if she could hardly believe that she was at home. For there, at the edge of the orchard, stood a summer-house so much like the one in Grandma Hinman's garden that Ellie almost expected to see Peter and Hannah Jane coming down the path.

"Isn't that fine?" exclaimed Will. "Barlay made it for a surprise for you. Mother told him just how the one in Grandma Hinman's garden was made."

And then Ellie remembered that Barlay's last words to her when she started on her journey to Hartford had been of a "surprise," something that she would like, when she returned home.

"It is what I wanted more than anything," said Ellie, looking admiringly at the little lattice-work arbor, and at the comfortable seat. "We can have tea parties here when the Chaplin girls come to visit me. I wish I could thank Barlay."

"What is that little white button pinned on your dress for?" asked Will as they turned back to the house.

"Oh! It's to remember something by," Ellie replied, looking down at Bertha's "rose."

Both Stephen and Will were very proud indeed over the fact that Ellie had carried Barlay's message to Governor Trumbull.

"The governor wrote Barlay that it was a great service," said Stephen. "I wish I had been the one to carry the letter."

"But suppose anything had happened to your bandbox?" suggested Will. "*I* think Barlay ought to have told you to be careful."

"Oh, I was careful," laughed Ellie. "Why, I didn't have a minute's peace on account of that bandbox," and then she told them of the loss, first of the bandbox, and then of Barlay's package. But she said nothing about the golden sovereign. She had resolved, however, that some day she would tell the young Englishman about it, and about Brownie and Joe, and of the happiness the money had given them.

Good news had come from Ellie's soldier father that very day, so it was a happy group which gathered in Barlay's arbor and listened to all that Ellie had to tell of her Hartford visit.

"And what was the very best of all your visit, dear child?" asked Mrs. Barlow.

For a moment Ellie was silent, and then she said slowly: "Well, I suppose the best of it all was really Grandma Hinman. But there were so many things: Hannah Jane, and Brownie, and the little Chaplin girls, and— What are you laughing at, boys?" she demanded, for Will and Steve were both chuckling quietly.

"Why, at you, Ellie. You think everything is 'best,'" said Stephen.

"Well, it is," said Ellie.